G R JORDAN

A Just Punishment

A Highlands & Islands Detective Thriller

This book was professionally typeset on Reedsy.
Find out more at reedsy.com

Contents

Foreword

This story is set around the prosperous city of Inverness in the north of Scotland. Although set amongst known cities, towns and villages, note that all persons and specific places are fictional and not to be confused with actual buildings and structures which have been used as an inspirational canvas to tell a completely fictional story.

Acknowledgement

To Susan, Harold, Evelyn, Pete, Joan, Wendy, Jean and Rosemary for your work in bringing this novel to completion, your time and effort is deeply appreciated.

Novels by G R Jordan

The Highlands and Islands Detective series (Crime)

1. Water's Edge
2. The Bothy
3. The Horror Weekend
4. The Small Ferry
5. Dead at Third Man
6. The Pirate Club
7. A Personal Agenda
8. A Just Punishment
9. The Numerous Deaths of St. Nick

The Patrick Smythe Series

1. The Disappearance of Russell Hadleigh (Crime)
2. The Graves of Calgary Bay
3. The Fairy Pools Gathering

Austerley & Kirkgordon Series (Fantasy)

1. Crescendo!
2. The Darkness at Dillingham
3. Dagon's Revenge
4. Ship of Doom

Supernatural and Elder Threat Assessment Agency (SETAA) Series (Fantasy)

1. Scarlett O'Meara: Beastmaster

Island Adventures Series (Cosy Fantasy Adventure)

1. Surface Tensions

Dark Wen Series (Horror Fantasy)

1. The Blasphemous Welcome
2. The Demon's Chalice

Chapter 1

J ane hobbled to the front door, barely able to support her own weight. Her hands were flung out on either side of the hall as she rocked from wall to wall, slowly making her way forward. The dressing gown flapped open and she felt the wind from the open door through her light pyjamas.

'Jane, where the hell are you going?'

'I'm fine, Hazel, sit back down and drink that coffee. You've done nothing but run after me and I'm grateful, but some things a woman has to do on her own or it just isn't worth it.'

Out in the driveway of their house, Macleod stopped and turned back to his front door. He watched as through it came his partner, Jane, her brunette hair and robust figure compromised by the injuries she had received from an accident with a bus over a month ago. She had made better progress than they thought she would, but then, her spirit was undeniable. Together with Hazel Mackintosh, breast cancer survivor and changed woman because of it, Jane had managed to get herself fairly mobile to the point that she could manage five or six steps at a time. But this charge outside the front door was at least three times further than she had managed before.

As she stumbled up to him, Macleod opened his arms and she fell into them. He held her up and found her beaming at him. 'You don't clear off for a day's work without a goodbye kiss from your babe.'

Macleod laughed at the word babe. His woman, yes, but babe. Being in his sixties and Jane in her fifties, the word babe was wholly inappropriate but then that was Jane. She could tease just at the right time and he found her at times outrageous, if always endearing.

'It's my first day back in a month, woman,' he said. 'Is there no leaving me alone?'

'Never, not with those younger women trying to get their hands on you.'

They both laughed and were joined by Hazel Mackintosh, forensic investigator until she had taken time off after her cancer treatment.

'I'll take care of her, Seoras,' said Hazel, taking the strain from him.

'Oh yes, time to crack open the gin. Cocktails, that's what you're missing.'

As he drove the car out of his driveway, taking the back roads out of the Black Isle onto the main road into Inverness, Macleod found himself breathing somewhat heavily. His last meaningful contact with his senior officers had been walking off at Fort Augustus and deliberately ignoring DCI Dalwhinnie. His line manager had sent a letter telling him to take a month off on compassionate leave to look after Jane, but he felt it was also a defensive manoeuvre, one to keep him and the offended upper echelons apart. What did he care? Retirement was not that far away.

Driving over the Kessock Bridge, he looked down on the football stadium to his left. The season had started and soon the place would be filled on Saturdays. Life just rolled on.

There was the usual delay in crossing the bridge as the cars congregated at the roundabout beyond the stadium until the traffic lights let everyone move on. There was talk of bypass lanes and that, but there was always talk.

The day was cool but crisp, autumn making its bid to oust summer and Macleod was delighted that the heat was going. He was happier in the cold, at home with the snow which was something for a man from Lewis. Twenty minutes later, he pulled the car up into a spot in the car park at the Inverness police station.

Rather than enter via the main door, Macleod skirted around to the rear and past someone smoking discreetly by a car. There was a time when you would have sat in the canteen and puffed away, but he was glad that these days smokers had to take their filthy habit outside. He had never smoked, nor drank for that matter, and maybe that was why he was in as good a shape as he was in his sixties.

Sneaking in quietly, he managed to avoid anyone and even tiptoed his way across the empty office that usually hosted his team, making his way into his own office. On the desk was a large cardboard box and Macleod looked at the front of it, seeing it had been delivered by a courier. He thought nothing of it and lifted the box to take it to his round desk where he held his more intimate team briefings.

He felt his shoulders give a little cry as he lifted it and fought hard to carry the box over to the round table where he unceremoniously dumped it. *That was a bit much for a first action*, he thought. *I hope they still have some decent coffee.*

There was a rap at the door. Through the frosted glass, he saw a figure he recognised.

'Come in.'

'You ready to go?' said a female voice. He turned fully now to look at the new arrival. A crisp and tight white t-shirt had an open leather jacket over it and was set off by a dark leather belt with some flashes on it. There was a pair of black jeans and boots with a flat heel.

'You look good, Hope. It's good to see you dressing your way and not to fit in.'

Hope McGrath, Macleod's DS, smiled broadly and then pointed at his tie and shirt. 'You still fitting in?'

'This is my style,' he retorted. 'From a classier era, you see.'

The pair laughed and then embraced. 'Good to have you back, Seoras. We're not flavour of the month after your cold shoulder of Dalwhinnie, but the DCI has kept most of it off our backs.'

'Well, you only have me part-time for the next two months, Hope, so you'd better be ready to keep carrying the can.'

There was another knock on the door and two faces looked in. One pushed a pair of thick-rimmed glasses up her nose while the man stepped forward and extended a hand towards Macleod.

'Good to see you back, sir,' said Ross and shook hands vigorously. He was rather shocked when Macleod stepped forward and embraced him.

'Thanks for everything, Ross; you did good down in Fort William. And so did you, Kirsten.' Macleod embraced the short blonde woman. 'You've all been more than colleagues, so I thank you. But it's back to the grindstone. So, five minutes time, McGrath, I want a briefing on what I've missed and then let's all get in here at ten for a plan of what we have before us.'

'There's nothing juicy on, Boss,' said Hope, 'only routine matters to look into. Thankfully, we've had no one with such brutal agendas this month.

As they cleared the room, Macleod looked at the box but left it and instead opened some mail. After a briefing from Hope, he then saw his team and planned out the day. A call from the DCI took care of another hour and after he had shot through a backlog of emails, he finally got round to looking at his box. With a pair of scissors, he cut through the packaging tape holding the lid down and carefully pulled back the cardboard flaps before looking inside. When he did, Macleod froze for a moment, staring at the contents, then he walked calmly to the telephone on his desk and rang an internal number.

'Miss Nakamura, yes, thank you for your kind wishes but I rather need you right now in my office. Yes, it's urgent. And Jona, bring a suit and gloves.'

Macleod held himself up against his desk, a distance from the box which was sitting opened on the round conference desk. Thoughts raced through his mind about who would have sent him such a package, but he was struggling to think of anyone who would give enough of a damn about him to bother. He had arrested plenty of people in his time, had some tough cases with really nasty individuals, but no one would send something like this.

The door was rapped lightly.

'Come in, Miss Nakamura. The item is on the round desk.'

Jona Nakamura was dressed in a white coverall and wore gloves. The hood hid her black ponytail, but Macleod saw the bulge. The woman who was from Asian descent, had a petite frame but she gave off such a positive ambience that Macleod often thought she should be employed to simply hang around depressed people who would then magically come back to a more positive frame of mind.

As she looked inside the box, Jona gave a small whimper and reeled back slightly before looking more deeply inside. 'Do you get a lot of these sorts of deliveries, Inspector?'

'No, in fact, never, if you can believe that. Can you identify the parts?'

Jona nodded and then stepped away for a moment. She walked to the window and opened it, sucking in a large draught of air. Having satisfied herself she was okay, Jona returned to the package.

'It's been broken several times to fit the box but that is a right leg of someone. Given the hair on the leg, most likely male, and given the genitalia that's been split in half, definitely male. Inspector, this is a quarter of a person.'

'I thought as much but why send a quarter of a person to me?'

There was a rap at the door. 'Come in,' said Macleod, 'but stay away from the conference desk.'

Hope walked in and stared over at Jona, her head over the box. Hope turned to Macleod. 'Sir, I have just received a call from a Detective Inspector Dalrimple in Wales. He received a package today and inside were parts of a body.'

'What parts?' snapped Macleod.

'Shoulder, arm, part of a head. Pretty barbaric. But he said there was a piece of paper inside and it had a name on it.'

'Really? Jona, is there a card in that box?'

'I think so, Inspector, I'll try and fish it out.'

Hope stepped forward closer to Macleod. 'My colleague said it was your name on the card?'

'Just my name?'

'Yes, just your name?'

Macleod walked over to Jona. 'What's on this card?'

'Hang on, I'll just get it.' Using a pair of tweezers, Jona lifted the card and placed it in an evidence bag. Then she laid it on the table beside the box. There was dried blood on the card, but it stated one name on it: *DI Seoras Macleod*.

'Flip it over, Jona, check if there's anything on the other side.'

Jona used a pair of tweezers to flip the card and there were words on the other side. The writing was small, so tiny that Macleod could not read it, but Jona stared at it closely.

'Justice that does not require punishment, or a punishment that is not appropriate, is no justice at all. You were meant to be our saviour, Macleod, not theirs.'

Chapter 2

Macleod looked through the frosted glass of his office wall from the side his team usually sat on. He had been pushed out to their office by Jona Nakamura who insisted on everyone getting out of the Macleod's office until she had completed forensics on the box. Feeling a little put out by this, although he knew it was the right decision, Macleod now sat in Ross's chair waiting for Hope to finish her present phone call. Stewart was busy on the computer already searching up links between Macleod and DI Dalrymple in Wales—cases they had worked, criminals arrested, places they had worked.

Hope set the receiver down and looked at Macleod with heavy eyes. There was a silence in the room which Macleod felt was unhealthy, but he knew where it was coming from. The team felt he was under attack in some way and that was giving the investigation a sense of foreboding.

'That was DS Lachlan in Kent, sir. He received an arm and another side of the head in the post. Again, your name was on a piece of card and no other message. The pathologist down there is looking at the pieces of the body and I have asked him to co-ordinate with Jona. I think you should make a call to the DCI and make sure we get to run this case as it's beginning in four different parts of the UK.'

'Four?' queried Macleod.

'Yes, sir. Just heard from Lachlan that a DS Munroe in Northern Ireland, Belfast to be exact, has received a similar item but this time the other leg and hip. With where they are, they had thought some of the dissident paramilitaries, but I'll ring them and advise what we know. But we need to bring this case to a central point. With your name and the fact that we are the only ones to have received a message, it should be us to take the case.'

'Of course, it should. I'll make that call. Ross, get onto our colleagues in Northern Ireland and get all the details about their delivery that you can.'

'Yes, sir,' replied Ross. 'By the way, do you know any of these officers who have also received packages?'

Macleod pondered the names. 'Dalrymple may have walked the beat with me. Lachlan is familiar, as is Monroe, but there's plenty of officers with these names. Get me a breakdown of their career paths and I'll see if there's a crossover.'

Macleod spent the next half hour briefing the DCI and discussing options before letting her go to organise a pulling together of the resources and evidence they had. By this time, Jona Nakamura had finished in Macleod's office and had retreated with her two assistants allowing the Inspector to once again take ownership of his room. Macleod instantly called a meeting at his round table and sent a request for Jona Nakamura to join them as soon as she could.

'Did we get the career records for the other recipients?' asked Macleod.

'Yes sir,' replied Ross, 'and I cross-referenced them, but it was not hard. You started off in Glasgow with these officers on the beat. At the time you were all patrolling officers but two worked in a different station to you, sir, which is why they might not be so familiar. Dalrymple worked with you but the other two were at separate but nearby stations.'

'Seems a bit random,' said Hope.

'It does until you look at arrest records. It was not easy, but I managed to get a list of who were called to arrests at the time,' said Stewart. 'What I mean is I looked at large arrests where you might have expected a pool of constables from several stations to attend in the area. I narrowed it down and by process of elimination, I think—'

A rap came on the door and Macleod asked the caller to come in. Jona Nakamura appeared, now without her white coverall and instead in a smart pair of green trousers with a quiet orange shirt.

'Join us, please,' said Macleod and offered Jona a seat.

Jona was slightly out of breath but she smiled at Macleod. 'I have a name for the victim,' she said delightedly.

'Kyle McAvoy,' said Stewart.

Jona looked shocked. 'How did you know?'

'The Inspector helped arrest him along with constables Dalrymple, Lachlan and Munroe. The arresting officer was a DI Forrester, but the report says that several constables carried the suspect out.'

'Who was he, Stewart?' asked Hope.

Macleod held his hand up to Stewart. Standing up, he walked away from the round table and stood at his desk looking out of the window to the station car park. 'Kyle McAvoy was one of the sickest individuals I have ever dealt with and I was fortunate enough to just be running the basics as a constable. I didn't have to investigate him properly, just assist. He was a child abuser and a killer.'

'How long ago?' asked Hope.

'What is it, Stewart, thirty years?'

'Record says twenty-eight, sir.'

'Really, that long. I suppose I had only been down in Glasgow three years after my wife had died. Still very green around the gills. McAvoy evaded capture for over six months after he had been identified as the killer behind a string of child and adult victims. When I say adult, they were usually under twenty-one.'

'Boys or girls, sir?' asked Hope.

'Both. Utter bastard. One of life's devils. The ones who make you think that there's no place for compassion in this world. Putting him down would be best, that's what they said. But after we arrested him, it went to trial; he was convicted and as far as I knew, he was still in prison.'

'Actually, he was released six months ago, sir. Was all done very quietly and under a new name.'

Macleod looked at the tablet in front of Stewart and scowled. These machines took away all the drama of memory. 'Well, he's God's to deal with now. May He have mercy.'

'That doesn't seem to be how our sender of the packages sees it,' said Jona. The Asian woman had sat quietly after being upstaged.

'Sorry, Jona, we kind of cut you off, didn't we. Please, what have you learnt?'

'Well, the fingerprints confirm that the body is indeed Kyle McAvoy and having spoken to my colleagues around the UK, I think we can safely say the man was hung, drawn, and then quartered.'

'What, like in olden times?' said Hope disbelievingly.

11

'Very much so. There are intestines missing. I believe the practice was to hang the victim but not in the drop fashion that we imagine. If you simply drop into the noose, the neck can break, and many died straight away in that fashion. Instead, you gently lowered them into the noose where they slowly choked and when they were close to dying, they were taken down and placed on a slab or a wooden frame. At this point they were pulled apart by the arms and legs. The skill was to keep them alive so that they saw themselves being cut up, intestines pulled out and the like.'

'Bloody hell,' said Stewart, 'that's gross. And you believe Kyle McAvoy suffered like this.'

'The early investigations indicate yes, but we can be sure when I get all of him to the morgue. As you can imagine, he's got a lot of travelling to do.'

Macleod was staring thoughtfully at the ground. 'What are you thinking, sir?' asked Ross.

'Jona, how strong would you have to be to do this?'

'If the person was not impeded with drugs or something of that ilk, or a serious injury, which at this time I can neither rule out or in as you can imagine, then it would be difficult. McAvoy, I think, is about six feet tall and he looks fairly strong. Again, it's hard to tell when he's not together.'

'Anything else from your investigations so far, Jona?'

'No, sir, but going back to the point I made earlier. The note talked about justice and it needing to be done in the correct way. But the note then seems to blame you, sir, for something.'

'I was their saviour, not that of the writers.'

'I assume we take that as your function as a police officer,' said Hope.

'But you were only doing your job,' Ross chipped in, 'so why

12

at you personally?'

'Maybe it's personal to the case,' Macleod answered. 'I mean that's how it sounds. I know there's no direct link but McAvoy's in the box with the note, so surely, it's to do with what McAvoy did and then how he did not get his just desserts in the sender's eyes.'

'I agree,' said Jona, 'it does feel that way.'

'Good, so here is how we start. Stewart and Ross, get into the case where I arrested McAvoy. I want a list of victims and suspected victims. Family members too. Let's get into the case in big way. I want you two with a complete knowledge of it. McGrath, work with Jona and get a hold of these cards and see where you get a supply like that. Also, these items were posted, so find out where and when. They have a tracked and signed for, because obviously you don't want any of our man going astray. See if the post offices have CCTV of our sender.'

'Yes, sir, and what shall you be doing?' asked Hope.

'If this is personal, and it does look like it, I'm going to try and remember everything I can about this case and what I did. Why would they know me by name? I had truly little to do with the case; I wasn't even a detective back then. So why me? Why would—'

There was a rap at the door and a man with fading grey hair stuck his head into the office. 'Apologies, but Miss Nakamura has a call from Kent. They said it was important.'

'Tell them I'm coming. If there's nothing else, Inspector, I'll take that call.'

'Sure, fine,' said Macleod, a little distracted. 'Oh, Jona,' he said as she was exiting, 'no word of this to Mackintosh, unless she comes into the office to work. I don't want it getting to Jane. She has enough on her plate.'

Jona nodded. After she left, Stewart turned to Ross, asking, 'Who was the old guy?'

'New start with the forensics, taken on to cover a gap in knowledge. He's older than they normally start them, but he has experience in the library, cataloguing and that. Apparently Jona lost her best two filers upstairs and the place was getting a mess, so she demanded someone new.'

'Can we get one of them?' laughed Stewart.

'What's that?' said Macleod.

'Nothing, sir.'

'In that case, away you go and become experts on the McAvoy files.'

As the pair left the room, Hope swung round from the round desk to face Macleod at his personal desk. Staring for a moment, she then took off her jacket and hung it over her seat. 'I'm ready when you are.'

'Ready for what?'

'All your memories from that case. You know as well as I do, the correct way to do this is for you to try and recall what you can and for me to record and prompt you for further as and when. You didn't think I was going to let you do this on your own.'

Macleod let go a slight grin. 'Of course not.' But then his face became more serious. 'Who goes to the trouble of actually hanging someone and then pulling them apart to then gut them and chop them up? Just the practicalities of it are staggering. I mean, imagine the space you would need.'

Macleod went round his desk and took up his seat. For a moment, his hand seemed to shake. 'Hope, if this is personal, and it looks that way, then I need you to look out for me, and my nearest and dearest.'

'Well, I did stay behind because I thought it might be worthwhile thinking about protection for Jane and possibly Mackintosh at the house. Your house is remote but easy to get to.'

'Thank you for your concern, but at this time I don't want Jane having to deal with anything else but her recovery. She's pretty vulnerable at the moment, never mind having to worry about myself or anyone coming to the house. All we have is a box and a body.'

'All we have is a murderer who has a beef with you. I'd say that's more than enough. There's a high likelihood that you are a target.'

'I don't see it that way, Hope. If so, why kill a criminal? They are angry at the criminals and maybe the system.'

'And yet they addressed you by name. You need to be careful with this one, Seoras.'

'Noted,' said Macleod rather abruptly. 'If you're going to insist on doing the recording, shall we get on with it?'

'Okay,' said Hope, and took out her pen and pad. 'Whenever you're ready.'

It was two hours later when they decided to take a break and Hope looked at her pad. She didn't even have a page full. Macleod truly seemed to know little about this case but then it had happened not long after his wife's death and maybe that was a factor.

Hope checked in with her charges during the break and found them both eyes deep in records and photographs. Ross said there was more to get out of the archive but he thought it might be a good idea for the Inspector and Hope to speak to the arresting DS at the time and get a view of the case from their point. Of course, that was provided they were still alive for they may have left the force some time ago.

Macleod came out of the office asking Hope if she was ready to go again but as he passed by Stewart's desk he stopped for a moment. On one side of the desk was a card, one that looked like something you collected or played in a game. It had on it a picture of a woman in cartoon form. Her outfit was ridiculous as no fabric could ever hold on to skin like that, so little and tight to the skin.

'What's that?' asked Macleod.

'Sorry sir, should have put that away.'

'What is it?'

'It's a collectible card, sir. It's Alliah, witch of the seven veils of Castronian, keeper of the powerful amulet of Darfone, ghost in the night, and Mistress of the dark.'

Macleod stared at the card. 'She obviously lives somewhere warm.'

'Oh, no sir, she actually lives in an ice palace. It's quite a costume.'

'Very . . . liberating,' said Macleod.

He turned to walk back to his office but heard Stewart say, 'It is, sir. I was thinking about it for the Comicon next month. Been a while since I wore an Alliah costume.'

Macleod turned and stared at Stewart. Involuntarily his mind pictured her in the outfit. And then he turned back to his office, quickly. 'I'm sure you'll be quite the talking point,' he said, but in his mind he fought to lose the image he had seen. *In my day you only dreamed of getting a girl to wear something like that. Now they do it voluntarily and for fun.* Part of Macleod was disgusted, and the other part left its comment at *Good for her!*

16

Chapter 3

I t took Hope most of the day to round up CCTV footage from the post offices around the country. Before contacting the specific force in each area, she had to wait for the post office to identify where each item had been posted. They gave her four different post offices, but all were in Scotland. Most of the branches were small and local, and Hope contacted the local area police to assist in the acquisition of the footage required. Aviemore, Banff, Lochinver and Portree—a widespread range of drop-off points.

Glancing at her team across from her, Hope sighed as she prepared herself to watch yet more footage from the post offices. From the labels on the posted boxes, she knew that the boxes from Lochinver and Portree were posted the day before those from Aviemore and Banff. The distance between each facility was at least two hours of driving, often much more, so in order for everything to arrive at the same time she knew they had to be posted separately but at times when the post would all leave on the same day. Hence, she realised that Lochinver and Portree were posted after the last collection from that post office.

Lochinver's post office was inside a shop and the camera used to record the screen from behind which the post office operated was not the clearest. Hope fast forwarded to the time of posting on the label and saw a man with a large coat come into the shop and appear at the window. A mop of black hair seemed to almost wrap around his face and with the high angle of the camera, she could not get a good look at his face. Carefully, she used the image software on the computer to enhance her view and then printed off a copy on the laser printer.

Walking over to collect the printed item, Hope thought how non-descript the image had been. The large coat shielded any view of the person's frame and hair and the camera quality meant there was little to see on the face. Sitting back down with her printout, Hope started on the Portree footage.

This time the image was clearer, but it was a woman who had dropped off the package. She was blonde, again the hair voluminous and so that it covered a lot of the face. The woman also did not turn her face to the camera, seeming to know exactly where she would be filmed from. Before starting on the third set of footage, Hope checked in with her team to make sure they were making progress and found them up to their eyes in the case file surrounding Kyle McAvoy.

The footage from Inverness and Banff had the same two figures from the other post offices but were just as unhelpful in identifying who had sent the packages. There was nothing discernible except for the height of the persons—around five feet ten. So, there was a greater likelihood of a man, but a woman was not a ridiculous idea either.

Hope took her findings to the forensics lab where she struggled to locate Jona Nakamura. Hope spotted the new arrival in the division. So far, she had not been introduced but the fading grey hair was distinctive, and the man almost seem to migrate to her in her time of need.

'Sergeant McGrath, can I help you?' Behind the man, Hope saw the rest of Jona's team beavering away at various desks.

'I was looking for Miss Nakamura.'

'In the morgue, Sergeant. I'm not sure how long she'll be. Would you like me to ring her?'

'I know where it is. I'm sure Jona won't mind a visitor.'

The man nodded and almost bowed out of the way. Feeling a little disturbed by the man, Hope walked the corridor to the morgue and knocked lightly on the door. After being summoned through, Hope saw Jona standing before a clean metal table with a leg in front of her. Behind her she saw the computer screen Jona was working from which had a split screen of three other morgues all with a forensic officer working at a body.

'Hi,' said Jona, not looking up from her work.

'Sorry to bother you but I was just dropping off the CCTV footage from the post offices. Nothing's clear but I wondered if you would take a look at it and see if you can spot anything more than me. I reckon the poster was about five feet ten, but I can really see little else.'

'I'll get on it,' said Jona and then turned around and muted the computer behind her. 'Got a bad feeling about this, Hope. Has a real personal feel about it. I'm worried about the DI.'

'You think they are going to come for him. They might just be making a point. The man on your slab is fully deserving of his punishment, is he not?'

Jona turned away and picked up a cup, drinking slowly but keeping her back to Hope. Waiting for her to finish and turn back, Hope felt the silence grow. 'Am I wrong?'

'Deserves to be hung, drawn, and quartered? They did it for

treason back in the day,' Jona stated quietly. 'An example to all others who would plot against the king. It's totally barbaric, keeping people alive to suffer.'

'Well, the man did interfere with children.'

'Maybe he was sick. Clinically, he was ill. Maybe he couldn't help it, like an alcoholic.'

Hope started. 'Are you trying to defend what he did?'

'No! Of course not. But you don't condemn the alcoholic for his actions. You try to help. You don't simply torture him so he doesn't do it again.'

Hope frowned. 'The alcoholic only hurts himself. This is different; that man lying there hurt a lot of people, scarred some irreparably. He was lucky we got him first.'

'Yes, he was. Some people are not so lucky.' Jona kept her back to Hope but she heard the Asian woman sniff.

'What's up, Jona?'

'One of my uncles was a man like this. He lived back in Japan. They got to him first. He didn't want to have the thoughts he had. There is another side.'

'Well, when it comes to kids, Jona, I'm afraid it's a little hard to see that.'

Silence filled the room until Jona unmuted her computer screen again. 'If you'll excuse me,' said the forensic officer, 'I need to get back into this. I'll get your footage examined and let you know.'

Hope left the room and wondered why Jona was so sensitive about this issue. Sure, it was her uncle but if Hope had a relative who behaved like that, she would have thrown them to the wolves, if not have dealt with them herself.

Since Jona had moved in with Hope to share the house, things had been great. Jona, often a sensitive soul, was nonetheless easy to live with. They ran together most mornings and did their shopping together. Indeed, Hope had to sometimes remind herself that Jona was only interested in being a friend as Hope would explore other possibilities if she thought different. But this was unlike Jona to be so stubborn and defensive on an issue. She had started disappearing off on certain days and had not told Hope where she was going, only that she was off to meditate. And when Hope offered to join her, she seemed panicked and refused point blank. There was no time to think about these things now, not with this rather strange case on their hands and Hope returned to her desk.

Having traced the packages to their posted locations, Hope decided that she would need to get the local officers to get an interview with the postal workers, to see if they could give a better description. All the items were paid for in cash so there was no help there. There were no stamps either as all were paid for at the post office, so the only label came from the counter printer. Maybe there would be CCTV outside the post offices they could tie into the strange characters who had posted.

It took Hope another hour of ringing around the various stations to organise what she wanted but by then she certainly felt better about herself. The tiff with Jona had knocked her off balance slightly. Hope might be forthright in her views but she was not without compassion. Maybe she should apologise.

As if on cue, Jona entered the office and made straight for Macleod's door. Hope stood up and watched Jona ignore her totally. 'Jona?' The Asian woman turned around, scowling. 'Look, maybe I overstepped the mark, sorry.'

'Yes, you did. I can't talk now; I have an appointment with the DI.' With that she turned around and headed for Macleod's door again but then swung round on her heel. 'Yes, about five feet ten, Hope. And no, I can't see much more than that.'

I must have really hurt her, thought Hope. Glumly she sat back down in her seat. Wanting something else to think about whilst waiting for the local officers to get back to her with their investigations, Hope looked over at her team.

'Ross, what's happening?'

Hope realised that while Jona and she had had their moment, her junior colleagues had kept silent and not said a word but underneath, she reckoned they would be itching to know what was happening.

'I've been trawling through the case of Kyle McAvoy. He was a particularly nasty character and had interfered with a large number of young people. The hunt for him was extensive and he was caught by a member of the community in the act with a child. The police responded and dragged him from a baying crowd. According to the reports, they were getting ready to string him up. Seems the boss was just one of the officers who had to grab him and take him out of the situation. Otherwise the DI had no real involvement in the case. He was, as he said, just arrived in Glasgow and had not yet become a detective. I've also been compiling a list of people who were affected by McAvoy's actions, or at least those we know of from the case notes. I'm currently tracking down addresses so that we can get them traced.'

'Good,' said Hope. 'We think the sender of the item was around five feet ten so filter all people who today are five feet eight to six feet and we'll start with them. When you have the full list, let me know and I'll send it down to Glasgow. Do you have any idea on the numbers we are looking at, just to give them an idea of manpower required?'

'Well I would say we'll have about a hundred affected in one way or another, as family members or victims,' said Stewart. 'With the height filter, maybe get that to down to twenty to forty. Until I get some records, I can't whittle them.'

'Understood, Stewart, keep on it. Anyone actually claim revenge according to the case notes, Ross.'

'Still working through but there are a few.'

'Tag them and we'll pay special attention, see if we can't narrow our field a little.'

Hope was drawn to Macleod's door opening and Jona walking out with a call of 'I'll see you later' over her shoulder. The woman was smiling and seemed lighter but then became more sullen as she caught Hope's eye. Clearly the apology was not going to be enough. One of Hope's favourite things about Jona was how sensitive she could be, capable of seeing things in many different layers. But in this case, maybe that was unwarranted. These sorts of people who caused such harm, especially to young people, deserved little sympathy. Jona would come round. Either that or they would just have to stay off the subject in the days to come. Still, Hope felt uneasy that things were not as smooth as they could be.

'McGrath, can you come in a minute?' shouted Macleod through the door. Hope got up and knocked on Macleod's door before entering. He was sitting, looking out of the window again.

'Is that all you do in the higher echelons—stare and think?'

'And I thought you had a taste of command. Sit down, Hope, I need a word.' Hope sat down and waited for Macleod to turn his chair around. 'Have you ever been involved in a case like this? Anything with a vendetta or similar against someone in the force?'

23

Hope shook her head. Maybe Macleod had forgotten but she had not been that long in Glasgow as a detective when she was bumped over to work with him. Yes, she was flying high in terms of her career, but her experience was nothing compared to an old hand like himself.

'No, Seoras, never.'

'Well, I have been . . . twice. Once was someone dropping rather nasty suggestions into beat officers' homes. Someone had felt they were unduly done by and decided that they wanted the officers' families to get a taste of fear. There was no violence except for the verbal kind. Another man actually tried to find and attack a DCI once. It was fairly inept but the reason I bring them up is the rather unsettling effect they had on the those involved in the investigations. I may seem to be taking this all in my stride, Hope, but that's because I need that team out there to function well and feel like they still have a leader and not a quivering wreck.'

'Are you scared?' asked Hope.

'Frankly, yes. Someone just butchered a man to send me a message. I mean, it's like a scene from a mafia movie.'

'Probably just a disturbed mind, Seoras.'

Macleod stood up and turned around slowly. 'It's a disturbed mind that bothers me. Someone who is deliberately setting out to frighten me would not be a problem. I mean, I've been intimidated before, plenty of times in my career; comes with the territory. But this is something else. And when does the next message come?'

Hope frowned. 'Next message? Who says there will be a next message?'

'Look at the card. That is not a complete message; that's someone lecturing, correcting the subject. Somehow, I have

24

erred, and he—if it is a he—wants to put this error of mine right. So, what is this error? Is it specific?'

'Well, you were part of the arresting team for Kyle McAvoy and some would say he didn't get what he deserved. In fact, I was talking to Jona and we disagreed heavily on this. I'm not going to cry if someone like McAvoy meets an untimely end. As an officer of the law, I will work to see the law upheld and due process ensues but if someone got there first, I wouldn't shed any tears.'

Macleod breathed deeply and Hope could feel the displeasure. 'There but for the grace of God go I, Hope.'

'You're not serious, sir? The man was almost like a wild beast from the case files. How can you even compare yourself to someone like that?'

Again, Macleod breathed slowly. Turning his back to Hope, he looked out of the window again at the rather unimpressive car park. 'I really need to get a better view than this.' And then he turned, looking directly at Hope. 'I have seen people who reacted to a scene and kill. I have had to pick up the pieces after a mother killed her child. I watched a man love his wife so much he destroyed what they had with his physical abuse. I don't excuse the behaviour but the forces that drive us are not so simple.'

'I thought the Bible demanded justice?' said Hope. 'An eye for an eye?'

'At least read it before you start with that nonsense, Hope; you're better than that. If you can get past the ticket to heaven theories, you'll find a life of compassion to all. Everyone. Even evil like this.'

'Sounds crackers to me, Seoras. You can keep that air-headed stuff.' She watched him start to shake a little and then he

25

breathed deeply again.

'You try and live it and tell me how when you've cracked it.'

There was a silence in the air that belied the tension. Hope could feel him simmering down but also found Macleod to be disappointed. Then he smiled at her. 'One last word and forgive the expression, but you're young. Time may teach you otherwise. I apologise if that's smug—it's just an observation.'

Standing again, Macleod walked to the door of the room and Hope wondered if he was going to throw her out and then rage about her inside his own office but instead, he simply pointed at the door.

'As I was trying to say, this kind of case has an effect on those who have to deal with it. And yes, I am scared by this. But we need to operate like it's a normal case and not get blinded by what's thrown at us. I will do this, too, but as the subject of the attacks, I may not achieve this. So, what I'm asking is that you keep an eye on the team but also an eye on the case, using that brain of yours to keep the line of investigation correct.'

Hope stood up. 'Always; it's what a second does.'

'And Hope,' said Macleod, stepping away from the door to let her out, 'when we first got teamed together, I may have underestimated that brain of yours, blinded by your looks, ascribing your rise to the top as their product. I apologise. It's not how I see you now.'

'I know. I'm still here.'

And then it hit her. She had been somewhat callous about things that mattered to him. 'And sorry for calling out your faith, Seoras. I do have a great respect for you even if I disagree with it all.'

'It's okay; we can take it.'

'We?'

'God and myself. He just carries himself an awful lot better.'

Chapter 4

As Hope drove down the A9 towards Glasgow, Macleod was aware that she was somewhat sullen. He had decided to visit the detectives who were interviewing the victims and others involved in the McAvoy case from all those years before. Macleod was not looking forward to it as he had made some enemies with how he had cold-shouldered DCI Dalwhinnie during the last case but the woman had betrayed him, not trusted his instincts and experienced detective nose, unlike Hope.

Macleod had initially taken a look at the detectives given over to the case and was annoyed when he saw the main leads, Grimshaw and Talent. Scott Grimshaw was nearly as old as Macleod and had been a DS on several occasions only to be busted back down each time for either sloppiness or outright bad behaviour. He was a dinosaur, a relic from a police force that had been somewhat misogynistic. Nowadays, he was lost in the tide of equal values and LGBT rights. Unlike Macleod, who had struggled greatly, Grimshaw had missed the bus and was not running after it. With a year to retirement, it was said the force had given up on him and were keen to simply pension him off as soon as possible.

But Grimshaw was not the worst of the pair; for as much

as he was what he was, he could be relied on to actually try to do some good. Tracey Talent was dirty and a survivor. They had never caught her, but Macleod knew what she was. Again, she was older and a bit of a looker for an older woman, at least that is what Grimshaw would say. No wonder he was happy to be paired with her. She had teased Macleod about his beliefs many times, in days when Macleod was more unsure of himself and leant on the doctrines and laws of his denomination rather than on the very God he claimed to follow. Both of them were reminders of poorer times and Macleod was not keen to engage with them. But work was work and this needed doing.

'You're very quiet, Hope,' said Macleod as they passed Stirling, looking to pick up the M8 shortly to Glasgow.

'Just driving, sir.'

'Keep an eye on Grimshaw; he'll have words to say to you. Especially after we stood up last time with the supposed terrorist. You're a prime candidate for him.'

Hope turned and stared. 'What do you mean by that exactly?'

'I mean, he's a sexist pig but he'll throw the charm on in front of a smart, sophisticated good-looking woman to get his own ends met.'

'I think I can handle a sexist pig.'

'Probably, but I'm just saying. And watch out for Talent. She's not clean cut, very dubious, and out for herself.'

'They're just running interviews for us. What can she do?'

'I don't know but just be careful, Hope. I know you can handle yourself, but this pair are old school.'

'Point noted, sir.' The tone was abrasive and Macleod shifted uncomfortably. He had enough on his plate without this attitude that must be coming from somewhere.

'What's up?'

'Nothing.'

'Nonsense. What have I done?'

'You,' emphasised Hope, 'have done nothing.'

Macleod took a moment and thought about the last twenty-four hours. Apart from his time in the station, he had only been home, helping Jane and Hazel Mackintosh and then had popped out for an hour late at night with Jona Nakamura for some meditation work. Maybe there was something in that.

'Is this about Jona?'

'Why did you have to start this with her? She skipped my yoga session because she was too tired when she came in. Said you had drained her, because of how deep you were.'

Macleod thought about the meditation work they had done and how at the end of it they had sat in his car talking through their lives, sharing things of note they were struggling with. Now he saw it. Hope had struggled with Allinson and then suffered the sharp end of that broken relationship. But Jona had moved in with Hope and they had been getting on famously until Jona had built this friendship that she and Macleod had.

'Sorry. She asked me. If it's an issue, then we'll stop.'

Hope stared out of the windscreen. 'You don't need to. It's fine.'

'It clearly is not. We'll stop.'

'It won't change anything. I'm just too shallow.'

'No, you're not. She just hasn't found the richness you have underneath. In fact—.' And Macleod silenced himself. He could not say that.

'In fact, what? Come on Seoras, what?'

'I should not say. I would be interfering.'

Hope thumped the wheel and then spun off the road to a

service station and drove the car fast and hard until she had parked it in a bay. Unclicking her belt, she turned to him. 'Interfering in what and how?'

Macleod turned and sat back trying to be as non-threatening as possible, in order to defuse Hope before the sharp comment to follow. 'You like her, and she knows it, but she is not interested in that way. I think she doesn't want to get too emotionally and intellectually attached in case it stirs you into looking for more. She doesn't want to lose a good friend.'

Hope collapsed back in her seat. 'But she still needs that level of intellectual attachment and so she talks with you because underneath, you're a complicated but sensitive man, Seoras. It's the hard exterior along with it that makes you attractive.' Hope realised she had said this out loud. 'Sorry, shouldn't have said that.'

'It's okay. Talk to her, Hope. Stop fearing what could happen.'

'But every time I get close to someone, it goes to crap.'

'We're still good,' smiled Macleod.

'But you're the boss.'

'Go and work for forensics then.' It was a comment Jane would have made but Macleod had seen it work. He saw Hope smirk and then she gave him a delicate punch. 'But in the meantime, Detective Sergeant McGrath, can we get to Glasgow and deal with this shoddy pair they've given us?' Hope fired up the car and they were on their way again.

The Maryhill station in Glasgow was busy and Macleod had to wait until DC Grimshaw wandered in to pick him up from the front lobby. As he approached, Macleod watched him staring at Hope who had her back turned. The man looked from Hope's bottom to Macleod and then screwed his lips up pretending to make an 'ooh' sound. As Hope turned back, the

31

face leapt into a friendly smile.

Grimshaw shook hands with them both and then ushered Hope on ahead and leant into Macleod. 'Good god, you're an old dog and a half. Must be sweet having that toddle up to you every day. Nice set . . .'

'Stop!' said Macleod and whispered to Grimshaw. 'You refer to my colleague in that vulgar way again and I will haul you up to standards and get you on a six-month enlightenment course.'

'Been on that twice. Worth it for a set—'

'Stop! I'll put it in plain English for you, Grimshaw. I'll haul you out to the car park and kick the tripe out of you. In fact, I'd let McGrath do it but you'd enjoy that too much. I'm a DI so behave like the DC you are. If it were up to me, you'd be on the beat full time until they could dump you. Understood?'

'Yes, sir,' said Grimshaw with added emphasis. He motioned for Macleod to walk ahead and Macleod could feel the gobby comments being made behind his back. Still, he had put Grimshaw on notice.

The Inverness pair were led by Grimshaw to an office where Macleod saw DS Talent sitting in a black skirt that was too young for her age. He could see the stocking tops when she shuffled in her seat and Macleod thought she looked like she was in a cheap movie. Her blouse was like something a twenty-year-old could go clubbing in and Macleod refused to stare, ignoring his primal instincts. Unlike Hope, the woman had no class.

Grimshaw made teas and coffee and Macleod noted that Hope got a clean mug while his was dirty on one side. The prime choice of biscuits was also given to Hope first. It was pathetic.

'We've produced all the witness statements from those closest to the case back then, but I think you may be out of luck. The only people in the height range are not about and certainly have had no contact with McAvoy since his release. Your forensics officer, Nakamura, said that McAvoy was dead forty-eight to seventy-two hours before the parcel arrived and we have only one person who fits the height of the post office deliverer and who was available without an alibi to kill McAvoy. And that man has a mental age of six. Poor bastard was scarred rather heavily by McAvoy although he was a bit cuckoo to begin with.'

Macleod rolled his eyes. He was a senior officer and yet her tone was sloppy. He could understand why these two had been assigned to help; after all, Glasgow had not received any of the pieces of McAvoy in the post. They no doubt did not want to get involved. If it came out about what had happened, then the media scrum would be a no win. There would be all the debate about how this was a fitting punishment for McAvoy and really why are we not dealing with scum in this way. So, best to have your disposable officers on it if any taint comes your way. A cynical view, but Macleod knew there was a large element of truth hiding in there.

'Do we know exactly how many victims McAvoy had?' asked Hope.

'Only who came forward. There was never a complete total and McAvoy admitted to nothing. He would just sit there and leer when being interviewed according to the investigating officer's notes,' said Grimshaw, passing a smile at Hope.

'Have you gone to social services to get any idea about the number or even any names?'

'Wouldn't be worth it,' answered Talent. 'It's not like today,

McGrath. Back then, you didn't come forward about stuff like this in case you got tainted with it, too. It was less of a victim mentality, as it was making you a figure. As a girl you would probably be accused of offering it; as a boy, the last thing you wanted was any homosexuality ideas around you, even if you were not the one who was. That's what made the investigation so hard and why they only nailed him on about five accounts. And that was because two of them died. Otherwise he would have had a much lighter sentence.'

'So, in terms of people who might have wanted revenge on McAvoy, the list whilst being very large, is also very much in the dark,' surmised Macleod. 'What about the families of those who died?'

'I spoke to Moira Barrett, mother of Karen, the sixteen-year-old girl who he killed after engaging in some very deviant stuff with her,' said Talent. 'It was just her, no father around; he had died abroad when Karen was young. Moira's dying of every vice going; she couldn't get her shopping never mind kill anyone. Hasn't the money to fund it either. So, she's a dead end.'

'And the Fanshaws have moved away,' said Grimshaw. 'They couldn't handle it because of the rumour their son was actually gay. So, upped sticks to Australia.'

'Did you check?' asked Macleod.

'Of course, I checked. They haven't left the country in three years.'

'So basically, we have nothing,' said Macleod. 'As I understand it, he was only released two months ago. Have you looked into the prison? Were there any enemies there? Who knew he was coming out? They usually try and keep that sort of thing quiet in cases like this.'

'I made the call,' said Talent. 'They said no one knew.'

'Did you go and visit? We have a body that's been butchered. There are people connected in prison who could do something like this for money, or just from bad blood. They may be the muscle and not the brains behind it. You need to go check, Talent.'

'And where did he go when he came out?' asked Hope.

'No idea,' said Grimshaw.

'Then get out and get an idea,' spat Macleod. 'Get yourselves down to the prison and start there. I want to know his movements before he died.'

'Okay,' said Talent, 'we'll take a run by tomorrow afternoon.'

'Get yourselves down there now! From what I see, all you've done is basically look through the files and get some of the obvious people in to talk to. Or did you even do that or did you send the uniforms out? It feels sloppy, Talent. There may not be much to find but I want to know it's not there. Now get in the car and get to that prison. I want a report tonight by nine o'clock. And then tomorrow, I want McAvoy's last movements traced. From when he left the prison to when he ended up in the boxes. Understood?'

'Yes, sir.' Talent rose, gave Macleod a stare, and waltzed out of the room. But Grimshaw stood up and then moved beside Hope, placing a hand on her shoulder.

'I think it would be wise to take someone else along with us. Could be a fair number of inmates to talk to.'

Macleod looked up, raising an eyebrow and was about to speak until he saw Hope stare back at him. He looked down at papers in front of him. Hope placed her hand on Grimshaw's and gripped it tight as she removed it from her shoulder. She dug her nails in hard and said, 'There's probably plenty of junior DCs available. If not, take a uniform to assist. I have work to do.'

Grimshaw's face fought to hide the pain of Hope's grip but he stepped away and she let her hand fall. 'Do you understand?' asked Hope.

'Yes, ma'am.'

Hope turned back to the table and waited for Grimshaw to leave but Macleod looked up and saw the man staring hungrily at Hope. She should not have engaged him for now he was more excited than ever. But Hope could handle Grimshaw, of that Macleod was sure and so he simply left it as the man slowly left the room.

'Not a great team, sir,' said Hope.

'No, Hope, I'm afraid it's the dregs. There's plenty of good officers down here but they have plenty to get on with. I don't think they'll find much either. It could be anyone of a myriad of people given what McAvoy did, and many we don't even know about. It's the connection with me I'm thinking about. That could be our line into them. I just pray we find it before they feel the need to send me another message. Somehow, I don't think the last one was a final word on the matter.'

Chapter 5

Jean Stewart had been a postwoman for thirty years but she never got tired of the daily round. That round was enormous for she delivered in the north of Scotland, from Strathy to Durness, along the most northern coast of the mainland. In winter, the roads were often rough—like the weather—and she would hop from her van to the door dressed in her waterproofs. Today was much more pleasant, although beginning to become a little autumnal.

She had come through Coldbackie and had taken the outlying road to Skullomie. The view of the sea as you approached Skullomie was breath-taking and always one of the best parts of her round and today was no exception. Buoyed by this, Jean sought out the few houses she had to deliver to.

She had noted that Marie from the last house in the village had a rather large parcel to be signed for. The woman was a bit strange and had moved in five years ago. Always nervous, Jean struggled to remember when Marie had not looked at her with questioning eyes, as if she were wondering why Jean was really here. If she pushed, Jean would have told her, 'money'. That was why most people worked. Whether Marie would be appeased with that, Jean doubted, but that was the thing about delivering here in the far ends of the world—you always got such varied characters.

After dropping a letter through the door for Mr Ferguson at the start of the village, Jean rounded the small number of houses and drove to the last of them. There was the rather clapped out white car which was sitting there every day. Jean had often wondered if the woman had ever gone out in it but then there was never any sociable conversation and Jean was none the wiser. As Jean stopped the engine, she waited for the head to pop out from behind the door or to appear from behind the house.

Marie was an older woman, but she was often in her dressing gown or 'loungewear' as they called pyjamas these days, and Jean had thought she would have made a great companion for an older man. She certainly could have lured one to her but maybe the woman was just too suspicious of any potential suitors. Stepping out of the car with the parcel and her small electronic pad for Marie's signature, Jean waited for the penetrating eyes to appear.

But none did and so Jean walked along the gravel drive up to the door of the white cottage and rapped on it with her bare knuckles. The door swung open and Marie saw the broken lock on the inside.

'Marie!' she shouted. 'Miss Robert?'

There was no response and Jean almost set the parcel down to investigate further but then Jean thought she would need to be careful. At least if she entered the house with the parcel and Marie appeared suddenly and in an accusatory tone, she could simply hand over the item and get a signature. After all, that was what she needed, a signature.

Stepping into the entrance hall, Jean was in new territory and she glanced at the multitude of pictures on the wall. It was somewhere by the sea but Jean did not recognise the place. As she tiptoed on into the house, she entered a cosy sitting room which had a number of framed pictures on the mantelpiece. What shocked Jean was that the pictures were all of an African woman, or at least a woman of that descent. She was dark skinned in the extreme and Jean thought she must be from middle Africa where the skin tones were the deepest. The woman had rich skin, and eyes that sucked you in with a warmth that was in extreme contrast to Marie. Vibrant clothes set off the woman's smile and Jean reckoned she could be a presenter on the children's channel given the warmth she was exuding.

There was a scurrying sound and Jean looked to the floor where she saw a rat. The package was thrown to the air and Jean leapt onto the sofa where she fell and landed back on the floor. The rat, maybe more panicked than Jean, vanished in a blur.

Jean picked herself up and rubbed a bruise on the back of her hand where she had fallen. *Let's get this done and get out of here*, she thought and grabbed the parcel again. Checking her pad was still working, Jean made for the door to the rear of the house again shouting for Marie. Maybe she was not in; after all, Jean had made a hell of a racket with the rat.

Turning into the kitchen area at the rear of the cottage, Jean first noticed that the light was still on. She then saw Marie lying on a breakfast bar at one side of the kitchen. Her hair was hanging over the end and she was in her dressing gown, except it was laid open. On top of her stomach was a metal cage. The cage was empty and as Jean approached, she dropped the parcel and threw up where she stood. Raising her now blurry eyes, wet with tears, she looked again but only managed to vomit once more. A rat ran past her foot but this time, she did not move, paralysed by a mix of horror and fear.

Jean stared, crying, and shaking like she was in a Siberia winter before she eventually managed to tear herself from the scene and ran out of the front door. As she exited the door, she screamed. And she continued to scream, begging for anyone. A man appeared from two doors up, Mr Jameson.

'Get someone,' screamed Jean. 'They've eaten her; they've eaten her!'

* * *

Stewart stepped out of the car and looked at the scene around the small white cottage. There were two paramedics in the back of their ambulance with a postwoman who was shaking and looked drained. White as a sheet, too. Beyond them, three police cars were surrounding the house and a uniformed officer stood looking grim at the front door. Milling around were several forensic officers and Jona Nakamura was in full swing with her white coverall's hood pushed back as she spoke with some of her colleagues. She clearly was not happy with someone, whatever they had done. After a rebuke, she chased them back inside the house and then strode over to Ross and Stewart.

'Some people are just are not as sharp as they should be. If you want to suit up, I'll take you in before we think about moving the body. According to the sergeant over there,' said Jona, pointing to a uniformed woman standing beside one of the police cars, 'the victim is Marie Robert. She's lived here for about five years. Be careful when you get inside; most of the rats have dispersed but there may be one or two left.'

'Rats?' queried Stewart.

'Yes, rats. They were brought here deliberately as part of the torture. Actually, maybe torture is wrong—you could say punishment. I'm not sure they were looking to extract any information or a confession. If not, it would be punishment. You might want to brace yourselves.'

Ross and Stewart donned white coveralls and placed plastic covers on their feet before following Jona into the building. Passing through the lounge to the kitchen, Stewart then stopped dead in her tracks before bolting from the room. Ross, after looking out of the lounge window to see his colleague was all right if a little shaken, returned and walked right up to the body on the breakfast bar.

Before him lay Marie Robert, dark hair hanging off the end of the breakfast bar and dressing gown lying wide open. Ross tried not to stare at the bloody stomach area before him but could see right through it. On Marie's stomach was a cage of metal. It had no floor.

'Pretty gross, even for what I normally see,' said Jona. 'Basically, I believe she was drugged or knocked out somehow and placed on the breakfast bar. You might be able to see where she was tied, not just by the hands and feet, but also across the torso. The cage was placed on top of her and when she was awake, the floor of the cage was removed, and its occupants started to find a way out.'

'I take it by occupants,' asked Ross, 'you mean the rats?'

'Probably starved. They would seek a way out or food and basically ate their way out. One thing to note was that the breakfast bar had a hole cut in it underneath her stomach. It would be a painful and horrible way to die. She'd eventually bleed out if the important organs managed to remain unaffected. Of course, she may have died of shock but looking at her, I think that is unlikely, the poor woman.'

Stewart returned to the room but kept a distance from the body. 'So, how did she end up there in that position?'

'Jona reckons she was drugged or knocked out to be placed there. There's also a hole in the breakfast bar beneath her which would have to be cut,' advised Ross.

'And there's one other thing to note, if you'll excuse the pun; there's another card, like in the box at the station.'

Jona picked up a small card in her gloved hand and brought it over to Stewart. Both Ross and she stared at it, seeing Macleod's name on it. Jona flipped it to the back. YOU SAVE RACISTS were the only words printed on it.

'I'm going to call the boss,' said Ross. 'Are you okay with us searching the lounge and around the kitchen?' Ross waited for a nod from Jona and having received it, he took Stewart outside for a breath of fresh air.

'You okay? That's not the norm, is it?'

'No,' said Stewart and then jumped as a rat ran past her. It tore off past the rear door of the ambulance and Ross heard a scream coming from the vehicle. Realising it was just someone scared of rats, he found the sergeant on duty and asked her for an update. Given the remote location, the uniforms had really been holding the fort. The sergeant had wanted to talk to the woman in the ambulance but she was having difficulty calming down. The paramedics had said she was in no danger, but she needed to be watched and until she was much calmer, they would rather the police did not speak to her.

Returning to the house, Ross asked Jona how long the woman had been dead. Twenty-four hours or so was the response. More than enough time for the killer, or at least the rat provider, to be far away. Stepping back outside, Ross asked the sergeant to go to the nearby houses, of which there were not many, and ask if they had seen anything.

Ross thought it best if Stewart search the living room and anything outside of the kitchen while he dealt with the areas closer to the body. After leaving the lounge towards the kitchen, Ross saw a dresser against the wall and began to pull out the drawers of the furniture. There were many pieces of material, possibly used for a hobby. It would make sense as Marie Robert was so far out here, that it was unlikely she attended that many clubs or evenings out.

Another drawer revealed photographs and Ross started to sift through them until he found two large packets of prints wrapped in a plastic bag. Taking out the first picture, Ross saw Marie, although she looked considerably younger, with a black woman. As Ross flicked through the photos, they were nearly all of the women and he noticed all were inside somewhere. There were no public photos. At the bottom of the packet, he found some more risqué photos. In saying that, they were sunbathing shots, in a back garden somewhere. It was just that there were not any clothes involved.

Ross took the photos into the lounge where Stewart was on her knees checking around the rear of the television. Ross tapped her on the shoulder and then asked,' Have you seen anything with this black woman?'

Stewart took one look and pointed to the mantelpiece. Ross saw pictures of the black woman although these were only of her.

'Did we get a background on Marie Robert yet?' asked Ross.

'I just rang through asking for assistance but I'm awaiting the reply. Having to use the airwave as the mobile signals not good. There's one of the constables outside awaiting the call.'

Ross nodded and began to search the kitchen. He had found nothing else of interest when he heard someone enter the lounge and he strode in to see if it was the constable from outside. Stewart was holding the airwave radio when he came in and the constable was looking a little put out as he stood close by awaiting the return of his device.

'Say that again.' Stewart was scribbling down notes as she was spoken to by a woman, presumably from Inverness station. 'Okay, thanks, I'll get back if I need more.' Stewart passed the radio back to the constable who marched back outside to take up his watch.

'Well?' asked Ross.

'It seems Marie Robert was jailed over fifteen years ago for a racist killing. There was a doubt about her guilt, so she got manslaughter, but the interesting bit is this. When she was arrested, it was in the middle of a council estate and there was almost an army of black people intent on getting to her before the police got to her. She was barricaded up in a flat and we had to go in and get her. Full riot team and all to get her back out. Quite a nasty situation.'

'Where was this?' asked Ross.

'Glasgow. When she got out it looks like she came up here miles from anywhere and kept a low profile. I guess there's people who don't forget.'

'True, but to do something like this—it's medieval. You'd have to have a pretty weird mind to execute someone like this. That's what Jona reckons, it was punishment.' Ross shook his head but then saw a smile on Stewart's face. She must have some juicy detail because the present situation did not warrant any sort of grin.

'You'll never guess who arrested her?'

'The boss . . . but that can't be right; he wouldn't have been a foot soldier then.'

'He wasn't, Ross, he was the lead investigator. He was the one who saved her life, getting uniforms to go in and get her. That's why his name's on the card. Seems he must have made a habit of hauling people away from baying crowds.'

Chapter 6

Macleod stepped from the car and took in the fresh air. Just over the edge of the nearby cliffs was the water and he could hear the seagulls calling. A stiff wind was now blowing and he pulled his coat around him. He could see Jona Nakamura organising her people to place a body bag in the rear of a wagon, no doubt transporting Marie Robert to the morgue. The name conjured up a lot of memories for him. It had been his first case where race had been an issue.

'Inspector,' called Jona, on seeing him, 'I'll get what else I can find to you as soon as I can, but whoever did this understands our procedures. The place is clean of all traces. Not a hair, or piece of skin as far as I can tell. Also knew how to disable the victim but also keep her alive prior to executing her.'

'Did she suffer?' asked Macleod, a tremble in his voice. Jona did not reply but simply nodded solemnly. 'Do you mind if I take a look at her?' Macleod continued.

Jona led Macleod over to the wagon and entered the rear of it before switching on a light and closing the doors. 'It's not a great sight, sir. Stewart vomited all over the scene on seeing Marie.' Macleod just nodded and Jona pulled down the zip.

The sight of her was indeed disturbing but Macleod was

focused on the face not the now disintegrated stomach. From time to time cases stuck with you and this one was one of the worst. They had come for her because they said she had killed a black man, this white girl, but in truth he had threatened to take away the one thing Marie loved, Liberty, his wife. They had fallen in love and at the time you really did not show that kind of love in the open. They had met in shadows, but the husband had found out and started to beat his wife on a regular basis. The police had made a cursory stop by but the beatings had continued. So, Marie killed him to free her lover.

But the world only saw black and white and she had been lucky as Macleod had been quick enough to realise who had murdered the husband and also where she was. Hiding in the laundry room of that tenement block, Marie Robert had been secreted for two days as the community hunted for her, along with the police. But Macleod had got there first and extracted her with a full riot team to face the law.

Marie's face was motionless and pale, a shadow of her. He had been a new DS, and this had been his first big catch as they put it. Despite how her orientation had appalled him back then, something he now regretted, he also fell for her courage and her absolute love of Liberty. Even after her sentencing, Marie Robert had remained with him. The others could read the case notes but they would never understand how personal this one was. He felt his hand grip tight as if he could strangle who had done this.

On exiting the wagon, Macleod was met by Stewart who started showing him the photographs they had found. He recognised the faces and when he saw the more liberal shots of the pair sunbathing, instead of a disgust which he had back in the day, he felt a warmth for Marie again. To love with such danger attached should not have been underestimated.

'We haven't found any trace of our killer. We believe he may have come in the night and set this up as the neighbours, the few that there are, saw nothing. Heard nothing either but they were about during the day.'

'It'll be hard to catch a break out here, Stewart. No cameras, no people—it's why Marie came here. Someone knew this case but only as an overview. It was played in the papers as a race killing but it wasn't. It was a love triangle that never got out. Marie Robert was Liberty Okusanya's lover and her husband found out. But Marie stayed silent about that after she killed him, so Liberty could walk away. Our killer did not know that so he or she could not have been involved with the case. Those close to it knew.'

'Maybe not,' replied Stewart, 'but they do know you. There was another card, same style as the last one. We might get a lead that way.'

'If it's like the last one then we won't. Jona says you can buy that sort of card anywhere and the ink is from a common inkjet printer. The killer makes their own cards.'

'So, we have nothing really, sir?'

'Maybe. Let's trace through the names of anyone involved with both cases and see if there are any matches. Just because they didn't know the intimate details doesn't mean they weren't around. But they also brought rats here so let's see if we can dig up any rat purchases recently. Did we catch any of them?'

'No sir, why?' asked Stewart bemused.

'Rats, like any other animal, have different breeds, I would guess. Maybe we can get lucky with a purchase recently. And that cage could be a custom-build job? Let's see if we can trace that.'

Stewart went off to locate the cage and Ross came over to his boss. On seeing him, Macleod thought again about Marie and how she had not been able to make her sexual orientation public. Ross was the same as Marie but at least he had that protection these days. As much as Macleod struggled with the whole concept of two men or women as a couple, he did at least believe they should be afforded the protection of the law. Ross was a decent person and of course he should have the same rights and freedoms as Macleod.

'Sir,' began Ross, 'although we have little to go on here, I was thinking about the murders. Each one was done as a medieval punishment. Hung, drawn and quartered, then rats on the stomach. It was punishment killing back In the Dark Ages, so I was wondering if our killer has a specific interest or had to garner one for this. Maybe we need to start looking at people who have taken out books from their libraries, joined medieval societies, or taken trips to the dark museums, those concerned with torture and the like.'

Macleod gave out a low whistle. 'That's a wide ocean to trawl, Ross, without getting everything caught up in your net. But do it. It may turn up something or confirm a later link for us. It sounds like one for Stewart. I hear she didn't react well to seeing Marie Robert.'

Ross shook his head and looked straight at Macleod. 'In honesty, sir, neither did I. I don't think this is linked back to the incident with the girl, when the suspect killed that guy in front of her. This is not like Fort Augustus when she froze. I wasn't far behind her on this one. I needed a good five minutes outside at one point, too.'

'Okay but let's get her doing what she does so well and start sweeping that rather large ocean you have put up.'

Macleod walked around the house and took in everything his officers had already seen in the hope that something might be sparked within him that would help the case. But there was nothing. Inside, his emotions were churning as he saw Marie's silent face in that wagon time and again. Exiting the house, he took a walk over to the cliffs to look at the sea. During his meditations with Jona, she said that the sea was always a good focal point—its repetitive nature and the fact that it was constant, always there. Sure, the water might recede, but it always came back. A bit like a police officer, especially a detective, thought Macleod. You can't keep us off the trail no matter how rough it looks. And this looks like it will be a rough one.

Hope tapped him on the shoulder. 'You okay, Seoras? Not like you to walk over to admire the view.'

'Jona's doing. She suggested it to me.'

'Another of your deep thought parties, was it?'

'No need to mock, Hope; this one was personal. Not that I was overinvolved in the case or with the suspects but there's things that went on which did not make the case files.' Macleod explained the love triangle and Marie Robert's sacrifice after she had killed Liberty's husband. 'Was my first really messy case where I only saw shades of grey.'

'Not our job to see it that way though, is it? She murdered him after all.'

'That she did, and she paid for it,' said Macleod. 'But what gets me is that this person is angry at me for simply arresting them, taking these people to our system of justice. Should I have simply struck them down? No, there's only one judge.'

'Two actually, sir, although I think the earthly one is being bypassed here. But you said this was personal and it all looks like you're being targeted so I recommend we put someone on the house, bit of protection for Jane, Mackintosh too, for that matter, since she's there.'

'No! It will scare the wits out of her as she's trying to recover from the injuries, Hope. She needs to be kept out of this.'

Hope walked around Macleod to stand in front of him. 'I disagree, sir; there is the clear potential for an obvious threat to your close ones and we need to put a vehicle up there to keep them protected. You are a target here and given the callousness of this killer, picking off people they probably don't know, your *family* needs protected. There's nothing linking these two deaths except you at the moment so it's time to be careful.'

'I won't run scared, Hope. It's a no for now but keep asking as this gets deeper.'

'You think it will get deeper?'

'Very much so. The killer hasn't told me anything yet. And as you say, he's talking to me with these cards, looking at things in my career. Well, you probably always wondered about my career before we met. Looks like you're going to get a good gander over it now. Go with Stewart and do some digging. Leave me and Ross to wind this up. You'll be better going over my career than me—after all, I'm a little biased.'

'Yes, sir. But I will keep on at you, Seoras.'

Macleod watched Hope walk away and thanked God for his team. With all that was going on and all that had happened in the previous months, his team had been a rock to lean on. Hope was developing as a dogged detective even if she needed a little push in the deduction stakes, but with Stewart on board that would be covered. And dependable Ross, a proper anchor if Macleod had to leave. He was getting too tired of this, but he knew as soon as the leash was yanked, he'd be off racing after that hare again, or at least striding along as best he could.

As Macleod walked back to the house brooding over things, he saw the forensic vans being packed with different items from the house. At the rear of the van the catalogued items were being placed into was a man akin to Macleod in years but with fading grey hair. Macleod recognised him as the man who had brought news of a call for Jona in his office. As he walked past, the man nodded.

'Is that nearly everything?' asked Macleod.

'Yes, sir. I think the boss has everything she needs.' The man coughed. 'Sorry, sir, you're the boss of course. Gets difficult remembering protocol in the new service.'

'Where were you before?'

'Librarian, sir, good with catalogues and records. This is a sweet job before retirement if somewhat grisly at times. But I'm doing what I find easy, so it's been a boon to find it.'

Macleod had thought about retiring himself to a different job for the last years but where would he go? He was a policeman, a sniffer dog, trailing through the bins of life and setting them back up straight, best as he could, for the refuse collectors to decide if the rubbish needed skipped or if it could be recycled back into the community. Maybe he was getting tired of it, but there was nothing else he thought he could do. Stay at home all day with Jane? He'd drive her bonkers, as wonderful as she was. And he hated any of those social sports.

'What's your name, sir?' asked Macleod.

'Cunningham, sir, Elijah Cunningham. I usually take the second name because the first is a bit over the top. Very prophetic name.'

'Well, nice to have you on board. I'm sure Jona wouldn't

have recruited you unless she was sure about you.'

Macleod turned and almost bumped into Jona who was walking towards the van. 'Oh, sorry, Jona, didn't see you.'

'That's okay, we are just about done so I'm going to get back to the morgue and get you the low down on Marie Robert, sir. If you need anything you can get me there. It's a bit of a trek back though.'

'Not so far our killer couldn't have come from south of Inverness and done the deed and get clear though, Jona. See what you can get me because we don't have a lot. And, Cunningham, you any good with catching rats?'

The man looked a little startled. 'Could give it a go.'

'Do you mind, Jona, before you go? I want Stewart to take a look at where they came from, pet shops and that, but we'll need to get the breed.'

'Well, if you don't,' said Jona, 'I can probably get that from the rat hair on the cage. But you need to understand, sir, these were not simply some rats bought in a shop. These rats were starved. That's why they ate through Marie Robert. As a way out and because they were hungry. You don't want to know the pain she would have been in.'

Macleod gave his thanks and took Cunningham over to Stewart who was looking for the rats before she left. Once they were united, Macleod began to think about the method of the killings. Medieval? What else could there be to come? Burnt at the stake? Hanging in a cage? Those were barbaric times. An Iron Maiden, spikes ready to crush into you as the door closed. Those things were the waterboarding of the day. We are just more sophisticated now. He took out his mobile. Time to see how Jane was getting on. He most certainly was not checking up to see if she was safe.

Chapter 7

Macleod grabbed the morning paper and threw it at McGrath. 'Read that! Just read that.'

Flicking the paper out so she could read the headlines, McGrath looked at the photograph of Macleod on the front page. It was an old one and he looked harassed in it. It had come from a trial he had attended in Glasgow prior to arriving in Inverness and he had been under pressure then. His face was angry, and a hand had unsuccessfully been put up to block the camera. Above the photo the headline read: POLICE HUNT THE EXECUTIONER.

'Well, they are accurate. These have been executions.'

'I don't care if they are accurate, Hope, that's not information the papers should have. Someone has given them details of the case. The boxes all arrived at police stations so only those inside the building would know what they held. No one found Marie Robert except us. Someone's been gabbing, Hope, opened their fat mouth for the money. Well, not on my watch. I want you to find out this mole and I'll take them down to the lowest rank.'

'It won't be from our team, Seoras. Ross and Stewart are solid, dependable.'

Macleod waved his hand vaguely in the air. 'I know that, I

wasn't suggesting it was any of you three. But it was someone up here. Both stories in detail. We need to check the uniforms that were up there. Forensics as well. Get hold of Jona and go through her team with her. I'll have a word on the quiet with some people I know in the papers. But I want you to head this up, Hope.'

Hope sighed. 'It's one of those things, Seoras. Don't you think it's a waste of my time when we have bigger fish to fry? I mean we have a double murder on our hands and you're a target.'

'Not yet I'm not and no, I don't think we should just let this go. This is about trust, Hope. They can think what they like about Glasgow back in the day, but we were a tight unit. And if you weren't, they soon sorted you out. The leaker would probably get a package on the way out the door these days, get set up for life.'

'I'll get on it,' said Hope. 'Have you seen the report from Jona on Marie Robert?'

'Yes. Drugged and then tied to the kitchen breakfast bar. A hole sawn out underneath and then she was woken up for the cage to be placed on top of her. She would have suffered greatly, Jona says. It's evil, Hope, that sort of thing. One thing to execute, clean and quick. But to make someone suffer—it's playing God.'

Hope stood up and turned for the door but then swung back round. 'I'll say it again, Seoras. I think this is aimed at you and you should have more protection placed on Jane. You don't want—'

'You think I don't know that! You think I don't see that the killer is antagonising me. But I can't worry her, and I also don't want our murderer to know he's got me worried. I want them to be more daring, easier to catch if they are. So, I need to stay cool, or at least give that appearance. Let them get sloppy. Otherwise what do we have?'

'Not a lot Seoras. Even the rats were a dead end. Could have come from a large number of pet shops. If they paid by cash, we have nothing. Those transactions we have traced have been put on a database because nothing has flagged about the individuals. I'll get your leak for you.'

Macleod watched Hope leave and then grabbed his mobile. Scrolling through the contacts, he saw the various names listed under 'press'. Libby Hughes' daughter. That was the one to go for. With something like this, he needed real discretion. It was a favour he did not want to call in, but the woman was in his debt.

It had been ten years ago and Libby Hughes had been set up to take the rap for a murder in the docks of Glasgow. She had been an innocent bystander but had been thrust in with a gentleman who was then murdered, and the knife placed in her hands. But Macleod had saved the prostitute from prison and had caught the scum who had perpetrated the act. Kylie Hughes had only been sixteen then but now she was a journalist and Macleod had seen her several times in the ranks of reporters. He had given her some bits and pieces, all readily available and accessible, but he had made it make sense and she had advanced as a reporter.

He grabbed his long coat from the stand where it was hanging and threw it on. Opening the office door, he turned to Ross. 'I'm going out, Ross. I'll be back in an hour. Anything urgent, you can get me on the mobile.'

* * *

The car that pulled up was an old Corsa and had nothing about it that said success. Macleod guessed that it was a functional car, capable of going anywhere and being unnoticed. You would not pay it a second glance, and it could sit in a street with its occupant observing things and never look out of place.

The driver's door swung open and a young woman in a blue jacket stepped out. Her brown hair framed a face that reminded Macleod of the woman's mother. Reminded, but it was not the same. Libby Hughes had worked the streets scraping money together to give her daughter a start in life and the work had taken its toll. But Kylie had no such worries. Her smile came from pleasing lips, a result of subtle lipstick and a willingness to engage people.

'Inspector, I didn't think I would get a call from you. Especially with all that's going on. It sounds grizzly.' The woman walked forward and gave Macleod a hug. It was respectful, simple, and was an acknowledgement of past help. Macleod gave a gentle hug back.

'How are things? Been a year since. You're looking well.'

'I am well,' said Kylie, 'but I miss her, Inspector. She was my closest friend. That doesn't heal easy.'

Macleod hung his head. 'No, Kylie, it doesn't. At least you had those years, I'm glad of that. She turned out a fine daughter.' There followed a silence while the two of them leant on Macleod's car side-by-side staring out at the water before them. They had come to a small car park just across from the Kessock Bridge, the large structure that dominated the area and that linked Inverness to the Black Isle. Macleod was currently standing at the old crossing for the firth, beside the Merkinch Nature Reserve. It was a place that he liked, open and with a splendid view, but also with only one way in and out which made seeing new arrivals simple.

'How did the press get details of the murders, Kylie? I kept it all supressed, not wanting to cause a panic.'

'I knew you would ask that, so I took the liberty of bringing the evidence we got served. It arrived in a brown envelope on the editor's desk.' Kylie handed over an envelope and Macleod took out a series of photographs that were inside.

'There was nothing else?' asked Macleod.

'No, but we kind of guessed what they related to.'

Staring at the first photograph, Macleod saw a leg in a box. Then there followed another leg and two pieces of a torso. A picture of rats eating their way through a woman's stomach came next. Marie Robert's face showed a picture of agony and Macleod had to put the pictures back in the envelope.

'Obviously, we couldn't print those,' said Kylie, 'but the boss decided to run the story straight away. It seems we were not the only ones to get that envelope. Most news outlets did. I think you're going to get a battering at your next press conference.'

'This came from the killer,' said Macleod. 'The rats haven't got through the stomach in a few of the pictures. The killer stood and watched her die. They're not making a point, they actually believe in what they are doing, deeply.'

Macleod stared out into the water as he took this point in and felt a shudder run down his back. But then he turned to Kylie and gave her a gentle embrace. 'It's good to see you looking so well. Your mother would be proud.'

'Take care, Inspector,' said Kylie and then gave Macleod a kiss on the cheek. 'If you ever need anything else, just ask. I'm always in your debt, you know that. You gave me back my mother.'

Watching the woman disappear in her car, Macleod felt a

warmth, seeing her as something he had got right in life. It was a hard but successful case and not all turned out so well. But then he thought of Marie Robert and it had not gone so well, now leading to her brutal death. That cold shiver ran down his spine again. Wrapping his coat about him, Macleod got back into his own car and drove back to the station.

As Macleod entered the office, Ross stood up and asked to see him in his side office. Macleod nodded and opened the door for Ross before placing his own coat on the hangar it had left barely an hour before.

'I've had the DCI on the telephone, sir, looking to speak to you. She's not happy about the press coverage. She's thinking of handling the press conferences given that the word is out about the "Executioner" as they are putting it.'

'No,' said Macleod, 'it needs to be me. The killer is goading me for whatever reason, so I need to be up front and handling it. I can't be away in the background. I'll speak directly to her, Ross, thank you. Oh, and send McGrath and Stewart in; I want to talk to you all.'

Ross nodded and disappeared for a few minutes before returning with his two female colleagues. Hope sat down in the main chair opposite Macleod while Stewart and Ross stood either side of her.

'I've just been talking to a press contact and there may not be a leak. The papers all received an envelope with photographs in it, pictures of Kyle McAvoy, at least bits of him in the boxes, and Marie Robert. What they don't know or can't tell is that the pictures of Marie Robert are as the torture happened. We know the rats ate through her, but the papers don't. Our killer stood and took photographs. The pictures of the body parts of McAvoy could be from our offices as far as the papers know.

But I've seen our pictures and they are not. They are pre-posting.'

'So, there's no leak,' said Hope.

'It appears not but keep your eyes and ears open. The DCI wants to start giving top cover, picking up the press conferences and that. So, keep her informed but I will be at those conferences, front and centre.'

'Is that a good idea?' asked Hope.

'Yes,' snapped Stewart. 'The boss is on the cards; he's being communicated to, so the press conferences are a way to communicate back.'

'I was just going to show a strong face, show I'm not intimidated. What do you mean, Stewart?' asked Macleod.

'Just that you can talk to the killer, send him messages in what you say. Put the pressure on, let them know we are on to them but not letting them know just how well.'

'Well, that'll be easy,' said Ross. 'We know nothing about them at the moment.'

But Macleod was on his feet. 'Yes, Stewart, good idea. They have been taunting me with the cards, stating they know something I don't; well, maybe we can feed how we are getting after them. We are close—hint at it.'

'Is that not risky if we don't know what they know about us?' asked Hope.

'How do you mean?' asked Macleod.

'Well, if there is a leak or they have insight into what we know and what we're doing they will know we are bluffing.'

'And what makes you think they have an inside contact, McGrath?'

'They know a lot about you. They sent the body parts to people you worked with. The victims chosen were from your cases at different levels of involvement. Yet they didn't know the cases intimately; otherwise, they would have known Marie Robert was actually a victim. I think it's somebody reading files. They found the victims, too. That means starting addresses. Former killers don't tend to advertise where they live.'

Macleod turned away to the window and looked out at the car park. The rain had begun and the rather poor view had become quite depressing. His hands went behind his back and he began to fidget with his thumbs as his hands were clasped.

'Sir,' prompted Ross.

Macleod spun round. 'So, what does the killer really want? Is it justice, served properly as they see it? Or do they want to punish those who have not enacted it properly? I guess we'll find out as more cards get delivered. But let's not have more. Find me anything we can hang on this killer, something we can start hunting him down with.'

The group broke up and Stewart and Ross left the room. Hope carefully shut the door and turned back to Macleod. 'Jane.'

'Not yet. They haven't come near me yet.'

'But they will, Seoras; it's in my gut. And by then it may be too late. Let me take care of it, tell her the DCI ordered it. I'll talk to the DCI myself.'

'No, you won't,' said Macleod. 'I need to be in control here; otherwise, our killer could see weakness and we want to rattle them, not have them thinking we are rattled.'

'But you are, aren't you?'

'I'm scared stiff with this one, Hope. I've never had a case like this, so personal. Vengeance for an arrest is one thing and even then, exceedingly rare. But this is the mind of genuine nutter. But a clever and calculating one at that.'

Chapter 8

Stewart was sitting in the canteen, enjoying a smoothie for her mid-morning snack when she saw Joshua Stewart pass by. They had been on the initial training course for new officers together and she remembered him due to the matching surnames. They had worked together on the course and had even studied together as they both were a bit odd when it came to working things out. Joshua had one of those minds that remembers everything and with Stewart's own skills at cross referencing, they had been a good team.

'Hey, got a minute?' shouted Stewart to the man as he walked past. The other thing about Joshua Stewart was that he stood six feet four tall and when they had been paired together, the look had been comical. But she had surprised many with her hand-to-hand combat abilities, despite her diminutive height and won the respect of an initially mocking crowd.

But the best thing about training had been being matched with Joshua and taking on that rather crisp frame. Despite moments of being detached and aloof, he was someone Stewart had connected with and she had been gutted when he went down to Edinburgh for a while. But in the last few days, she had noticed him about the station and today he had finally passed her by in the canteen, carrying a pint of orange juice.

Looking around him, Joshua Stewart took the seat next to Kirsten Stewart and then laughed as she looked at him. At first, she did not know why but then she realised she was pushing her glasses back up on her nose. He had often teased her about that at the training school.

'Still doing that,' Joshua laughed. Kirsten blushed and Joshua held up a hand. 'Sorry, embarrassed you. How are you, Kirsten?'

'Good, DC Stewart now. Yeah, I'm good.' And then there was a silence. Kirsten stared at the man before her and simply smiled causing a similar reaction back. Eventually, Joshua Stewart stood up.

'Sorry, Kirsten, I have to run; there's a missing man we're after. The DCI wants us back on the dot. It's been chaos all morning. But good to see you. I mean, really good to see you looking so . . . good.'

Good, thought Kirsten, *sounds promising*. Stewart wanted him to stay but really, she needed some sort of justification. Instead she simply blurted out the first thing that came into her head. 'Who's missing?'

People went missing most days and they turned up fairly quickly. If the DCI was taking an interest, then the man must have been missing in unusual circumstances. Maybe there would be something to chat about, if only briefly.

'Michael Hillier. Not been in his house for the last three days, missed all his appointments, doctors, podiatry, and not been seen at the gym. He was a regular workout freak.'

Something was clicking in Kirsten Stewart's head. Looking absently past Joshua, she delved into her mind, recounting details of different cases and pondering on pictures and sheets she'd looked at. And then it hit her.

'Father Alasdair McGovern.'

'No,' said Joshua, 'Michael Hillier, like I said.'

Kirsten stood up and was looking directly into Joshua Stewart's chest. 'No, Joshua, that was his previous name. The man was a priest. At least the one I'm thinking of was. Have you a photo?'

'Come with me,' replied Joshua and turned for the door. He led Stewart to a large office, one she was familiar with and saw the office of one of the Detective Inspectors at the far end. But inside, she saw DCI Dalwhinnie talking to someone. Kirsten felt like sticking her head inside her shirt. After the drama at Fort Augustus, her DI and DCI Dalwhinnie were barely on speaking terms.

Joshua Stewart's desk was neatly ordered but contained a large number of piles of paper and a pristine stack of photographs. The top image was of a man in his seventies. The hair was thin and grey, and the face was lined with thick wrinkles. But Kirsten remembered a face that looked younger but had the same haunting eyes.

'That's Alasdair McGovern,' Kirsten said pointing at the picture. 'I don't care what name he is going by these days, that's Alasdair McGovern. He changed his name, more than once if I remember and I think Michael Hillier was one of the changes.'

Joshua Stewart lowered his head so he was level with Kirsten's face and smiled. 'You don't change, do you? Never forget a detail.' Kirsten basked in the praise. 'You'd better come with me and tell the DCI.'

Kirsten's face fell. The last thing she wanted was to be in front of Dalwhinnie who saw Macleod's team as loose cannons, even if they had been right. Maybe it was the higher echelons lambasting Dalwhinnie for her part in the case, but she was harbouring a resentment that was only matched by Macleod. At least, that's what it felt like.

'It's fine; you tell her,' said Kirsten. 'Get you some brownie points.'

'And then she asks further questions and I look like an idiot because you know the groundwork not me; no way, Kirsten, come on.'

The office at the end seemed to loom as it got closer and Stewart felt a lump in her throat as Joshua rapped on the door and then opened it.

'Chief Inspector, I may have something.' As the two Stewarts entered the room, Kirsten felt like she was under scrutiny by Dalwhinnie, who glared at the new arrival. She was sitting on the near side of the desk with another man behind it. He was DI Frasier and he smiled as they came in, a complete contrast to Dalwhinnie.

'And what's that?' asked Dalwhinnie.

'I was talking to DC Stewart in the canteen and she believes Michael Hillier used to be a priest by the name of Father Alasdair McGovern.'

'Really, and how do you know this, DC Stewart?' Dalwhinnie was looking directly at Kirsten with fierce eyes.

Kirsten swallowed but then did as she always did when confronted. Her head dipped, she pushed her glasses back up her nose and stared back. 'I've been looking into DI Macleod's previous career due to the case we are involved with at the moment, as he is quoted by the killer at the scenes of crime. I was just asking Constable Stewart what he was involved with and he mentioned Michael Hillier by name. I recalled that was a name now used by Father Alasdair McGovern. Having seen a photo of Michael Hillier, I would say it is the same person although a lot older.'

'When was Macleod involved with Michael Hillier?' asked Dalwhinnie.

'The Inspector was in Glasgow and it would have been maybe twenty years ago. As I recall, the priest had taken money from a community fund, something which was destined for children in hospital, and when the community found out they started a witch hunt. The Inspector took him away from their baying hands, as the newspaper put it.'

Dalwhinnie stood up and looked at Joshua. 'Stewart, go get Macleod and ask him to join us here. If DC Stewart is right, then these may be interlinked cases and the DI and I have much to discuss. DC Stewart, Kirsten isn't it? Go and get whatever you know about this Alasdair McGovern.'

Kirsten Stewart disappeared out of the room, quickly followed by Joshua and as soon as they left the office and were in the corridor, she took Joshua to one side.

'I'll go get him and tell him what's happened. He'll be down shortly. Let me do it because Macleod won't like another section summoning him, especially Dalwhinnie. He'll give me the rounds of the houses for not bringing him in first rather than telling her. Come along, but let me speak.'

Joshua nodded and Kirsten took a moment to look at him. In the few years since they had last seen each other he had only got more handsome. But there was no time to stand and stare and she led the man to her own office where she saw Ross raise an eyebrow. With a flick of her head, she indicated he should follow and saw Hope in Macleod's office with the DI. Rapping the door, she waited for the curt 'Come in' and then opened it.

'Stewart,' said Macleod, 'and who's this with you?'

'Constable Stewart, sir, working with DCI Dalwhinnie's team on a missing person case which I believe is relevant to our investigation. Joshua was also on my early courses with me, so we got to chatting in the canteen. They currently have a Michael Hillier missing, an elderly man.'

'And?' queried Macleod.

'Well, sir, I believe, and I have seen a photograph, that Michael Hillier is the new name for Father Alasdair McGovern. You arrested him over twenty years ago—'

'Yes, I did, and you think he's been grabbed by our killer. Good work, Stewart. Go and tell the DCI I am coming to see her, and that I am requesting . . .' Macleod stopped talking and stared at Joshua Stewart. 'And you are here to fetch me. No phone call, no polite request. She actually sent a lackey to get me.' Kirsten could hear the anger in Macleod's voice. 'After all that she didn't do last time, you thought she would have a bit of humble pie. Just tell her I'm coming, Stewart,' snapped Macleod.

The two Stewarts looked at each other and then back at Macleod. 'I don't care which one of you,' stormed Macleod. As the pair turned for the door, Macleod called them back.

'Constable Stewart, Joshua, I think Kirsten said, sorry about that. Delighted to meet you. You'll have to forgive me, lot of history. Please advise your boss that I will be there shortly. And your own help is much appreciated.'

With that, Macleod cast a look to Kirsten who then cajoled Joshua out of the room. Once outside, she heard Joshua whistle.

'Blimey, what the hell happened between them?'

'You've only just arrived in Inverness, but everyone else

knows. The DCI didn't back Macleod on a murder hunt, the recent one with the terrorist incidents that weren't. Instead she went with the terrorist branch opinion and we nearly lost more people to the killer. Our team nearly lost a few of us when we had to take the killer down alone. Macleod's partner was gravely ill in hospital and Macleod had to come running from her side. That's a potted version but it covers it. So, take it from me, Joshua, keep your head down low and don't get in the crossfire.'

Kirsten looked up at the man who was staring back in disbelief. 'Were you okay?' Joshua asked.

'No,' said Kirsten, 'I haven't been okay in the field for a while. But this team is like my family and we were there for each other.'

'If you ever want to talk about it, Kirsten, we kind of had an understanding before at the training. Maybe I could help.'

Stewart looked at the man and she felt like she should say yes, engage him in his kind offer but she knew the last thing she wanted with Joshua was to sit down and have long meaningful conversations. She wanted to frolic around on a beach, play fight before a large fire and let off all the steam and rubbish that had built up in her life.

Kirsten placed her hand on Joshua's chest and shook her head. 'No, but you can take me to the cinema this week. We'll have to bring my brother because I haven't organised a sitter, but you won't mind that, will you?'

'No, I'd love that.' said Joshua. 'I'll go tell the boss and we can all prepare for World War III.'

Chapter 9

'So, we are saying that Michael Hillier could be a potential victim for your killer?'

'That's correct,' said Macleod.

'Well, it seems a bit slow of your killer; they seem to strike reasonably quickly. We haven't had anything from them so I'm not so sure,' said Dalwhinnie. 'Maybe it's just a coincidence.'

Macleod looked at those assembled in the office and wished they were all absent so he could deliver the verbal tirade the woman deserved. There was a time when she had followed his instinct but since she was further up the ladder, she seemed to begin to doubt whatever he was saying.

'Or maybe he just needs time to perform this particular torture. We are dealing with someone very calculating and precise. Orderly in mind. If they have Hillier for a long time, it will be for good reason.'

Macleod saw Dalwhinnie stare at him but Hope interjected. 'How does this affect the situation? You were dealing with a missing person, so I presume you went through the usual searches with a police search and rescue officer?'

'Yes, the POLSAR conducted the initial searches but then they closed down the searching of known haunts, last positions, and friends and family, of which there were not many.

We've been trying to look into known associates and track him down from that end. But we've had nothing. We were starting to look into the longer-term issues of his past but had only got started on that. As a former priest, that brings us a number of issues, especially if he has a criminal record.'

'And it suits our killer. He stole from his own community as a man of God. In the eyes of our killer, I'd say that would mean a stronger punishment than the basic ticking off he received,' said Macleod.

'I'll agree with you there,' said Dalwhinnie. 'Let's open up the search a bit more, try some camera recognition, and see if that helps.'

'Stewart is good in that field. I suggest getting Ross and Stewart onto that. Was there anything else at his house? Was it gone over by forensics?'

'No,' said Dalwhinnie. 'It was searched but we were looking at a missing person not a potential murder victim. I'll contact forensics.'

'Miss Nakamura's done all the forensic legwork on our case, Chief Inspector. I suggest you ask for her again, keep it consistent.'

'Well, of course, Macleod.' Dalwhinnie bit her lip as if she were about to say more but she thought better of it and instead looked towards Constable Stewart. 'Joshua, if you join DC Ross and keep me appraised of developments. I'm giving you this one, Macleod, but if you realise that it's not tied in with your case, I want it right back.'

'Yes, sir!' said Macleod curtly.

With the meeting over, Macleod's team returned to their office and Macleod asked Hope to accompany him to the missing man's house while Ross and the Stewarts began collating together any CCTV footage that might be useful from the area.

Michael Hillier lived in a house near the banks of the River Ness. Whilst trees blocked the view of the river, the area was reasonably flush, and his dwelling made Macleod wonder if he had continued his love of money to acquire it. There was a lush green lawn and a large house in that generous red brick that dominated the area. The windows were not double glazed but the older single pane with sliding frames. A great black door gave a foreboding impression to any would-be caller.

Jona Nakamura was there with her team and a constable opened the door to Macleod. Outside, the sky was overcast and a light drizzle had begun. Inside, the house was warm, the product of timed central heating and Macleod saw a hallway full of knick-knacks and antique furniture. Entering the lounge, a wooden fireplace dominated a dark room that had a bookcase with a multitude of leather-bound volumes. None of the books looked like they had ever been touched and seeing the titles, Macleod realised these were not today's best sellers but from a time when having your own library was a necessity for every well-to-do man.

Hope entered the room having made her way upstairs initially. 'Nothing out of place, sir. Looks like he had planned to be about. No space where a suitcase should be. There's dirty laundry in the basket.'

'What's that over there?' asked Macleod, pointing to a glass tank. Hope walked over and then stood still. Inside the tank was large black snake.

'Looks like a pet, sir. There is a lid on the tank. I guess I'd better call animal welfare at the SSPCA. Although I think they can go a long time without food.'

'But there's nothing put aside for it, and no one's coming in to check up on the snake. It doesn't look like he was going on a trip.'

'No sir, but it's far from conclusive,' said Hope. 'I'm not convinced Michael Hillier is a target yet.'

'Why?'

'Because, frankly, I reckon the killer would rub your face in it. They seem to want to engage you. And Hillier's crime is petty. Not like the murders committed by the others.'

'Marie Robert was not a murderer, Hope, just a trapped woman.'

'Yes, sir.' Hope turned away and began to look in the kitchen for more clues. There was plenty of fresh food in the fridge and dirty dishes in the dishwasher. Macleod joined her in the kitchen and began to shake his head.

'Nothing of note. Okay, Sergeant, get some uniforms and get this place searched top to bottom and see what we can come up with. Remember anything looks strange, get Miss Nakamura to look at it.'

* * *

Kirsten sat down in her seat and opened the video app on her computer. It was going to be a long afternoon of looking at CCTV footage from the local area in an attempt to find their man. Inside, she was glowing and keen to get on with the week so she could be taken to the cinema with Joshua. There were no guarantees but they had exchanged some close moments during training days before they had gone to different areas. Now he had moved to the highlands, maybe there was a chance for something more. Kirsten had hoped Ross would have placed herself and Joshua together to look at the footage, but he had been sent to collect some more while Ross was going to join Kirsten in this afternoon's endeavour.

'Okay, coffees are here, so let's get cracking,' came Ross's shout as he entered through the door of the office. After placing a large coffee in front of Stewart, he took up a position just behind her shoulder, slumped in a chair. *You can tell Macleod's out of the office*, thought Stewart and pressed play on the screen watching the comings and goings in fast motion. Every now and again as something caught her interest, she would slow the footage down but then speed it up again as something interesting became nothing at all.

The day rolled on and three coffees later Stewart wondered if her eyes were beginning to zone out from the screen of their own will. She could hear Ross's chair squeak as he lay back further on it. Everything was saying this was a waste of time. And then Stewart sat bolt upright.

'There! That black car. I've seen it before.'

'It's a black Corsa, Stewart; we see them all the time.'

'I mean in the footage, Ross. That same one. Look at the number plate.'

'It's fairly indistinct, can you read that?'

'I can read the last three letters. I could previously. I'm telling you, that's a repeat customer.'

Ross sighed. 'It is a pretty busy road. But go on; go back and find the car and how many times it's there.'

Stewart heard him stand and stretch while she began scooting back through the footage. There were five days of footage all up to when Michael Hillier had disappeared. And Stewart wondered if Ross was right. It was a busy road and maybe this was just someone going about their daily business and nothing important. But then that was how she got results, chasing the bland and obscure.

It took Stewart another hour to bring in all instances of the black Corsa and she smiled at Ross as he sat down to review them with her. She knew she was on to something and he would soon, too.

'Ross, take a look. The car is there on three occasions every day. Never the same time, always something different. Like a scouting trip but not wanting to be seen.'

'Anything else on the number plate?' Get any more letters?'

'No. It's only as he turns the corner that I get anything at all. But it's a black Corsa and three letters. There can't be that many to choose from.'

'Okay, I'll run it and see if I get any matches,' said Ross. 'Meanwhile, see if you can see who's inside the vehicle. Check if it changes. You might have something here, Stewart. You'll be the toast of the boss tonight.'

'And I win what for that? Peace for five minutes?'

Ross laughed and disappeared out of the office, leaving Stewart alone with her screen. As she worked at blowing up the images, Stewart became less aware of the office around her until someone tapped her on the shoulder.

'Excuse me, but I was asked to drop these files on the Inspector's desk. Is it okay to go in and drop them or do I need to give them to you?'

It was the new man from forensics, here to help with the filing and that. 'Hi, sorry you gave me a start. Just leave it here and I'll drop it to him. What's your name by the way?'

'Cunningham, Elijah Cunningham, ma'am. Pleased to meet you.'

'I'm DC Stewart, in case you are coming over regularly. I

don't want you tapping my shoulder like that again, gave me a right fright. But thanks, Elijah, and welcome.'

'Well, thank you, Miss, exceedingly kind of you to say so. Best get back to the lab.'

And with that the man was off and Stewart returned to the pictures before her. Because of the angle of the CCTV camera, the person always appeared in shadow and was hard to identify. But it did look like a male figure. At least that was something.

Ross came back in with a sheet of paper and sat down beside Stewart. 'Okay, so there's three black Corsa's with those last three letters on the number plate. Two English addresses and one Scottish address. I've got some southern friends looking into our English ones so let's get going on the address of our one. Oh, did you get any good shots of the driver?'

'No,' said Stewart, 'he's always in shadow, almost as if he knew. But I do think it's a *he*. I know we have had our imposters in the past, but I think it's a man.'

'Good stuff, we'll run with that and see what the address brings us. We're still a long way off proving the car has anything to do with the disappearance, but it does look like a generous coincidence.'

* * *

Hazel Mackintosh stood before the cooker watching the pan of soup bubble slowly. The idea of a tin of leek and potato soup disgusted her but for her current landlord, it seemed to be one of life's pleasures. Jane was sitting in the sunroom at the rear of the house and half dozing, a side effect from the tablets she was on. The accident where Jane had been hit by a bus was now in the past, but the effects were still very prominent.

Hazel poured the soup into a large mug and walked through to the sunroom to give Jane her dinner but she was asleep, snoring lightly. Placing the mug on a small table beside Jane, Hazel retired to the front of the house and stared out of the window. There was a winding drive through trees to the house and she tried to see the road that passed by at the drive's beginning. It was just out of sight and she decided to take a stroll to the end of the driveway, as much for air as out of curiosity.

Wrapping a jacket around her, Hazel realised that she no longer thought about the clothes she was wearing. Although never a fashion guru, she always liked to have a style and prided herself that she could turn a head or two. She had turned Seoras' head but the man was too upright to have acted on it. And now she was caring for his partner as Jane completed her rehabilitation. As her feet crunched on the stone path, she realised she was jealous of the woman in the sunroom. Each night Hazel went to bed alone, while Jane had him to cuddle up to.

Was it particularly Seoras she wanted? Well, he seemed to be the best if unavailable candidate around at the moment. It was not like she was desperate for sex, just someone to share life with, someone to curl up to, to tell her she was still a real woman. And that brought her back to the crux of what was eating at her. Her mind wandered to the surgery she had had, the day she had lost part of herself. Seoras still made her feel like a woman. As much as he obviously noticed a change in her appearance, he still treated her like the bustling professional she had been. And that was so attractive.

Shaking her head, she tried to clear this fog of thought that was distracting her from the fresh air she had come for.

Stepping off the stone drive, Hazel stood behind a tree and breathed in deeply. She had almost lost all of this. The cancer, now in abeyance, had threatened to take away the simple joy of life and she was going to grab what she could before it inevitably came back in her later life. Well, it always did—there was no point not being real about it.

Something flashed up ahead and Hazel instinctively moved behind the nearest tree. Peering from behind the pine, she saw a car at the end of the drive. Because of the curvy nature of the drive, whoever was in that car would struggle to see her. A light blue, the car looked like a Toyota, but Hazel struggled with the make. She was great at identifying them from tyre tracks and in photographs in work but there she had her comparison files to assist her. Here she was simply digging out shapes of cars from the back of her mind.

But she had been involved with police work for most of her life and learned a trick of two. Returning back to the house she took up a green wheelie bin and began pushing it up the driveway but keeping her eye on the area where she had seen the car. If someone came closer and in an open fashion, it was probably press. Vultures but harmless to her right now, at least physically. They might want a picture with all that Seoras was going through with the latest case. But if they stayed hidden, or crept up, then she would have a different issue on her hands.

Reaching the end of the driveway, Hazel left the bin to one side and could clearly see the car now parked just along from the entrance. There appeared to be no one inside and her eyes began searching the area around her. Turning back around, she began to walk back along the drive, but her eye caught something on her right. It was the slightest flicker of colour, but it was movement.

Hazel stopped and stretched her arms out as if tiredness had hit her and she was fighting back. She slowly turned around, breathing in deeply, like this was the most natural thing in the world. As she turned, Hazel saw the figure off to the right and the camera it held. Her face showed no emotion other than the pleasure of taking in the air and she breathed deeply as if soaking up the wood that surrounded the house. But with the corner of her eye, she was judging the size of the person.

She suddenly made off in the direction of the person, before dropping to her knees as if there were a piece of rubbish on the ground. There was no offending item, but the action had the desired effect. The figure bolted and ran for the car. A few seconds later, she watched it drive off.

All of a sudden, she could feel her shoulders shudder and a chill ran down her. Was it the press or was the person something more sinister? Hazel had been involved with too much of life's nastier side to simply dismiss the incident and as she walked quickly back to the house, her mind chewed over what had happened. On stepping inside the house, she locked the front door before making her way to the other two access doors of the house and locking them as well. Once completed, she checked on Jane but found her still asleep,

In the front lounge of the house, Hazel picked up the telephone and called the Inverness station asking for detective Inspector Macleod.

'Macleod.' It was hard to describe but it was like she suddenly felt stronger when she heard his voice. Despite the situation, the man brought a strength, maybe a level of protection. Something inside became warmer for hearing his tone. And then a pang of jealously swept over her as she thought of Jane in the next room. Moving out was something she needed to do before she lost control of these feelings she had for him. No one deserved where that could lead to.

'Seoras, it's Hazel. Yes, Jane's fine, but there's something you need to know . . .'

Chapter 10

Macleod looked at Hope, his neck muscles tense. For all that Hope had warned him and despite all his experience, the realisation that someone had been up and around his house with a camera was still genuinely disturbing. As soon as Hazel Mackintosh had telephoned, Macleod had called Hope into his office and asked her to assign the house protection, whatever she thought was needed. He was unsure that he could judge correctly the required protection given the house occupants.

'It's not the easiest house to protect but I have two uniforms up there permanently. I've asked one to patrol through the woods every hour and for the car to be sitting near the entrance. But it's an unmarked car and we're changing it daily through the unmarked cars we have.'

'Good, Hope. I spoke to Jane and said that with the current case we just need to keep the press away, but Mackintosh is aware of the possible real threat. I've told Jane to keep doors locked and that if she's outside it's best she has Hazel with her. I'm only glad she doesn't understand the potential threat because she's spooked enough thinking it's just the press.'

'Getting back to the case, sir,' said Hope, 'we've managed to identify a black Corsa that was near the scene and Stewart also got a partial number plate. There's only one match in Scotland, in this area, and two in England. The forces down there have confirmed those cars have not been away from the area recently and their owners don't have any connection to our incidents. Ross is out at the address of the Scottish match now with Stewart. Might not be anything but we'll see.'

Macleod turned away and Hope watched him clasp his hands behind his back, twiddling his thumbs. He then turned back around and sat down, grabbing some paperwork before throwing it onto the desk in disgust. 'I feel so blind, Hope. We have nothing. I'm a man for the hunt but we haven't got a sniff yet.'

'We will, sir. Let's just see what Ross gets for us.'

They sat in silence for a moment until Macleod's telephone rang. He spoke abruptly and then placed the telephone down. 'It's Dalwhinnie; she wants us both. Didn't say what but she sounded spooked.'

Hope allowed her boss to go ahead of her and they tore along the corridors to Dalwhinnie's office where they found the DCI alone. She was sitting at her desk, which was clear, something that Macleod's never seemed to be. There was only one item spoiling the clean top and that was a birthday card. On the front an elephant greedily ate cake while a frog played a trumpet.

'This just arrived for me, Macleod.'

'I take it that your birthday is not upon us, sir,' said Hope.

'It is not, Sergeant, but the front is far from the worst of it, McGrath.' Dalwhinnie opened the card and inside was a photograph. A teenage girl with a Latin tinge to her face sported thick, curly black hair. She was smiling broadly but the eyes seemed to be distant, as if she were unaware of the world around her.

'Carmen Tate,' Macleod spat. 'She's behind bars.'

'No, she isn't, Macleod. She was in hospital for treatment and was snatched or absconded two days ago. Not been seen since. Look underneath.'

Macleod pulled a glove from his back pocket and carefully opened the card. Inside was a message scrawled in blood and he found it hard to decipher the writing. Hope looked over his shoulder and carefully read what she saw.

'Punishment must be appropriate and always have an edge to it. What does that mean?'

'It means that Ross had better be getting somewhere fast with his car tracing or we will have another body on our hands,' said Macleod. Turning to Dalwhinnie, he asked, 'Has Miss Nakamura been informed?'

'Not yet, I called you first. I'll get her now.'

'We need to keep this quiet,' said Macleod, 'the press will be all over it searching for people.'

'By the way, who's Carmen Tate?' asked Hope.

'It was a case from way back which I was running,' said Dalwhinnie. 'Carmen Tate was a mentally challenged individual who had a habit of stealing babies. Unfortunately, once she took them, she didn't know how to look after them. There were three deaths before we got hold of her. It was tragic as in a lot of ways all she wanted was to care for them, but she had no idea how to do that. They sent her to prison but the hospital kind.'

'But that's not what our killer is on about,' said Macleod. 'You remember, Dalwhinnie, the crowd was after her. The girl was huddling in the shed, a crowd around her. If that young priest had not telephoned, they would have had her, and strung her up. But we got her first. Our killer reckons we didn't give her the correct punishment.'

'An edge to it,' said Hope. 'What's he mean by that?'

'Blade, some sort of weapon. Beheading?' suggested Dalwhinnie.

'Maybe a guillotine,' said Hope, 'that has an edge.'

'But we have no *where*,' Macleod said abruptly. 'And building a guillotine is quite a job. So far, it's been bloody but simple. The hanging and the drawing were away from us. The rats were just in a cage. A functioning guillotine is a work of art and easily noticed when buying parts. I doubt it will be so elaborate. It will be simple, brutal, and effective. Our punishments are medieval. But we need a *where*.'

'I'll check with Ross and see how he's getting on,' Hope said and left the room.

'Ross? Is he onto something?' asked Dalwhinnie.

Macleod shrugged his shoulders. 'Shot in the dark, sir.'

* * *

Ross stood with Stewart looking at the black Corsa parked on the driveway of the house that was located on the edge of Milton of Leys. The village was on the outskirts of the Inverness conurbation and afforded a view of the Moray firth. The houses were all recently built and this three-bedroom house looked like it had never been lived in. Ross peered through the window and found a living room with little to distinguish it from a show house. There were no family photos and no DVDs or music CDs around. Everything looked like the house had been bought and never lived in.

'Who did you say it was registered to again?' asked Ross.

'The car is in the name of Dermott Vaughn, as is the house. I've put a call into records to see if they can find out more about the name.'

'Well, it's certainly our car. But the house doesn't look lived in at all.'

'We could get a warrant,' suggested Stewart.

'Let's try the neighbours, first.' Ross walked across the driveway to the house beside. One of the things that Ross did not like about new builds was the fact that they all seemed to be stuck together with next to no gaps in between. Older houses had larger spaces, and a bit more privacy. He could put up with a faulty fusebox to not have his neighbour breathing down his neck every time he went into his garden.

Ross pressed the doorbell of the next-door neighbour and waited patiently as he heard a voice shouting for someone to be quiet. As the door opened a small face, only two feet from the ground stared up at him followed by a young mother who placed a hand on her child seeing the man at her door.

'Sorry to bother you, ma'am,' said Ross, holding up his credentials, 'police conducting some routine enquiries. I was wondering about the owners of the house next door. Have you seen them recently?'

The woman reared up a little. She was wearing jeans and a floppy cardigan and had a distrustful look on her face.'

'Is he in some sort of trouble?'

'Not as far as I'm aware,' said Ross, being truthful but saying nothing.

'I think he's away. I haven't seen him for a few days.'

'And what's his name?'

'Dermott. Mr Vaughn, pleasant enough but not that long here. Keeps himself to himself but a good neighbour. Soon shout if you've missed your bins and that.'

'And the car, does he use it a lot?'

The woman pulled the child behind her as the boy started making faces at Ross. 'Well, you have to. Unless you get the bus but we're pretty far up here. Gets a bit windy, too. I certainly use mine.'

'Does he drive any other cars?'

'No, not that I know of. But he's a friendly guy. So, what's this all about? Anything for me to worry about?'

'Not that I'm aware, ma'am. And thank you for your time.'

The door closed quickly behind Ross, but he saw other neighbours at their windows in the close. Part of him laughed.

'Any use?' asked Stewart and Ross shook his head.

'Away at the moment, it seems; pleasant guy, good neighbour. Nothing untoward. Maybe we should look at a warrant, but we haven't got much on him. His car's just been in the wrong place.

'Well, I've just been on the mobile with records and the name is an interesting one. There's a character who has changed his name by deed pole several times. I've asked for the lists to be sent to me for chasing up. Could be hard to tie them into this guy though.'

'Well, we should have a photograph coming soon. I got hold of the DVLA for details on any driver registered to this address or with this name. We'll see what it brings.'

As the pair got back into the car, they both felt a vibration: a text message arriving to their mobiles. There was one simple statement: A9 TOWARDS AVIEMORE. YOU'LL SEE THE CARS.

* * *

Macleod fidgeted in his seat as Hope drove the car past the waiting traffic. Uniform had managed to close off the road both ways on the A9. This was causing significant problems as it was the main route to Inverness from the south and routes around it were hard to find that did not involve a significant detour. But there was no choice given what they had been told.

Driving up the hard shoulder, Hope eventually cleared the traffic, and then drove the last three hundred metres to where a number of police cars were sitting in the middle of the road, some on either side of the dual carriageway. As she parked, Macleod stepped out of the car and walked at pace to the nearest constable who nodded politely and pointed to a gap in the trees across from the roadside. Macleod stepped over the central reservation, negotiating the silvery metal barriers. Hope hurdled them with alacrity, but she still felt she was chasing her boss.

In front of them at the roadside, stood a number of uniformed police, including a sergeant who was looking the worse for wear. As Macleod looked at his eyes, he saw there had been tears of some sort and he wondered what was about to face him. The man said nothing but instead pointed with a finger and Macleod looked into the clearing beyond the trees.

The first thing he noticed was the tall spike rising up from the ground to about twenty feet high. It was a dull rusty colour but had a silvery joint about halfway up and at other parts, indicating that it had been put together in sections. But then he saw the foot.

It was a red shoe that stuck out in the autumnal colours, scarlet as it was. Following the shoe up, there was a leg and then a bare torso of a woman. The spike re-emerged through

87

the top of the shoulder and Macleod found himself having to turn away for a moment.

'Bloody hell,' said Hope and Macleod saw her almost stumble with the shock of the image.

'Get everyone back,' said Macleod. 'Keep a good perimeter until forensics get here. McGrath, get hold of air traffic and advise them I would like no one flying over here at present but make it a good radius, couple of miles if you can. Thank goodness, it's a fairly cloudy day.'

As he watched the rest of the force spread back, Macleod stepped over the barrier at the side of the road and walked the fifty yards to where the spike was placed in the ground. He forced himself to look up and see the white backside that was pierced. A mop of black hair fell from the head which was now tilted to one side. Walking around the spike and then further out, Macleod was able to see the face of the victim and felt a tear come to his eye. He knew who it would be, but he dearly hoped it would not be so.

The last time he had seen Carmen Tate was in a hospital and she had been very endearing. After working on the case where they had to deal with a killer of children, he had come to the point of seeing her as a victim too, a poor soul whose actions caused such harm but who never intended to hurt anyone. He forced himself to look at her and under his breath he said a silent prayer, asking his God to take her to him. He hoped she had not suffered but the evidence to the contrary was right before him.

And then the body fell another foot down the pole. The sudden motion caused Macleod to reel and he fell over a stone, landing on his backside. His breath was broken, and he rasped for air as the image made the bile in his stomach start to rise.

He felt tears in his eyes and then a hand began to pull him up.

'Let's get back to the road, sir. Jona will be here soon with her team; we should leave this one to her. I take it that is—'

'Yes, it is. Poor Carmen,' Macleod blurted. And then he stood up tall and drew his tissue from his pocket. Quickly, he blew his nose before wiping his eyes and he wondered if they looked red. It didn't matter.

He was about to walk away when he saw a small bag on the ground. It was the size of a child's handbag, a toy really, but it was made of plastic. Macleod took out a pair of gloves and opened the bag, finding a card inside. He held it up and read his name on one side. On the other side was a simple message: JUSTICE DONE TO AN ANIMAL OF THE HIGHEST ORDER.

'She was a child, nothing but a victim herself,' cried Macleod to the air. And then he turned to Hope, waving the card at her. 'God's to judge, Hope, not us, you hear me, not us!'

Chapter 11

Macleod stood with Dalwhinnie looking at the body of Carmen Tate being brought down from the pole it had been placed on. A series of pulleys and a small crane had been employed but the descent was still undignified. At the centre of the effort to recover the body was Jona Nakamura and the senior Fire Chief from Inverness. Many of the fire brigade looked pale and some had even shed tears. Jona was not looking very well but as ever she was taking control of the situation. Once the body had been recovered, she made her way to Macleod.

'We'll take the body back for the post-mortem, but my guess is she was drugged, had the pole forcibly inserted and then was lifted. It is a large pole and I think it's also sectional, easier to move about. But if a single person did this they would be of a reasonable strength and would have used ropes and pulleys. Certainly, it could not have been done in an area with a high volume of people without being seen. My guess is it was completed here at night and then the morning traffic spotted the body.'

Macleod nodded and turned to Dalwhinnie. 'We still have Hillier missing so the next *torture* could be imminent, sir. The black Corsa owner, Dermott Vaughan is a good bet, so I'd like to use all necessary means to apprehend him.'

'Of course, Macleod. I'll help get that warrant for his house. What other lines do you intend to pursue?'

'Well, he built that pole, so he'd need to fabricate, or have it made, so we check all the metal works, fabricators. We'll canvas the area round here see if anyone saw anything but to be honest, there's not a lot of houses to see anything. The CCTV that is on the road doesn't go that far off it, but we'll try and see who was on the road, see if there are any number plates we should be aware of. And then I think we should contact anyone who I have arrested or been involved with in the past who might been considered to have got off lightly.'

Dalwhinnie sniffed. 'Long list, Macleod. We can't protect them all.'

'I'll get on,' said Jona, taking her leave and Macleod stood with Dalwhinnie as their people worked around them.

'You okay, Seoras?' Dalwhinnie asked in a low voice.

'No. You try hard to sort things, you trust it to our system. It's not perfect but it is at least generally fair. But this, this is summary execution. This is barbaric. And why on earth me? Tell me that. I'm trying to remember people from the past, grudges, but that's what they usually are, grudges, not righteous avengers.

'But this I do know. Someone has a lot of information about the cases but not the whole scoop. You and I knew Carmen's background. We understood her mental issues but it's not common knowledge. And as for Marie Robert, very few people really knew how she had been a martyr of sorts. So, we are dealing with an information digger but someone who doesn't get too close personally to fully understand the issue.'

'Well, it doesn't seem like much, Macleod, but I got your

team wrong before when you dug out things no one else did. I'll back you to the hilt on this one, Seoras. This cannot go on.'

There was a chill running down Macleod's back with the words and as Dalwhinnie walked away, he felt very alone. The car seen at his house was coming to his mind time and again. Yes, they had protection up there, but this killer had been ingenious. He wanted to create torture of the medieval kind and he had done so. This latest killing was evidence that the murderer would find a way to re-enact whatever they saw as necessary.

'Sir!' It was Hope and she had a confused look on her face. 'We've found Hillier. He was in a pub in Inverness and was spotted by an off-duty constable. He had been on a bit of a bender and was simply absent from home. Apparently, the landlord said he drinks a fair bit, wonders if he just crashes in people's houses because he's often leaving with different people. But he's safe.'

Macleod did not smile but rather simply grimaced and stared at the spot where Carmen Tate had been hanging. 'Did we get played, McGrath? Did the killer intend to be spotted near Hillier's? If so, how did he know we had bitten?'

'I don't know, sir. Are you sure that's not a stretch; maybe we just got it wrong about Hillier?'

'McGrath, where's Stewart?'

'Doing statements from the motorists that may have seen things as they passed.'

'Pull her off that. Tell her to come here and collect me. We're going back to the station to trawl up some potential targets. You stay here and round this up. You can keep Ross with you. I also want any descriptions you can get of the black Corsa driver, as much of a picture as you can.'

'Sir,' said Hope and went to turn but Macleod grabbed her shoulder and leant forward, whispering.

'I'm too close to this, Hope. I think they are threatening Jane, that there will be a punishment for me somewhere down the line. I need your clear head but understand me, someone is seeing more than they should here. The killer is messing with me and they know what they are doing. I can't say that I'll keep my detachment for this one. So, it's falling on you, Hope. I need you with this one.'

'I'll get them, Seoras. I don't like you being treated like this. I've got your back.'

'Looking after your boss,' said Macleod, 'thank you.'

'Looking after my friend,' said Hope, and smiled. Her hand grabbed Macleod's. 'No one's going to lay a finger on you.'

The intensity of the moment made Macleod blush, but he nodded and then stood up straight as she let his hand go. As Hope walked away no one could have told the intimate pact that had been made.

It was an hour later when Macleod sat down behind the desk of DC Stewart and watched Kirsten type away on her keyboard. She was running some sort of cross-referencing piece of software and Macleod had no idea exactly what was occurring but then that was why he had brought someone of her talents onto the team.

'So, what are you looking for, sir, exactly? How do you want to narrow the field down? At the moment I have over one hundred potential victims on the books according to your case histories. Without having some sort of restriction, we are going to be swamped in chasing up everyone.'

Macleod breathed deeply. Although Stewart could carry out the cull of potential targets quickly, it would be his restrictions that could keep someone safe or leave them open to an attack. 'Okay, Stewart, let's start by reducing all potential victims by having only those with a one-hundred-and-fifty-mile radius of Inverness. It does seem to be the centre of the attacks.'

'That's basically Scotland, sir, except for Shetland; maybe we should say fifty miles.'

'Would that have picked up Marie Robert?'

'No, sir, let's say eighty. That leaves out the central belt but just reaches Aberdeen and the north coast of the mainland. Eliminates the islands, too.'

'Good, so how many does that reduce it to?' asked Macleod. 'Twelve, sir.'

'Only twelve?'

'Well, most of your arrests were in Glasgow, sir, a few more towards Edinburgh. I've also tried to eliminate those that were not contentious and were minor offenses.'

'Okay, so of those twelve, is there any pattern about them?'

Stewart drew her breath in sharply and Macleod realised she was not used to having someone to hand hold while she worked. 'They are contentious and are in the local area and have you at the centre of them, sir. That's our pattern.'

'Let's take a look and see if there are any that seemed like poor sentences. Anything where we were hoping for a tougher jail term. Or any placed on the psychiatric wards.'

'Two were sent to psychiatric wards or prisons. They are out now in their own homes having been rehabilitated. The others went to normal prisons and served their time. If we can get into the detail of the crimes, we should see if there were any particularly violent uprisings against the arrest, or where communities were coming after the murderers.'

Stewart typed away and Macleod saw the screens flash by as

she read details he struggled with. Sitting back, she pushed her glasses back. 'I cannot find any with you being in the middle of a rough arrest, sir. I mean, it can't happen that often in a career, can it?'

'More than you would think, Stewart, more than you would think. Especially the really ugly murders, or those with kids.'

* * *

Ross sat in the car while Hope went inside the coffee shop and brought out two coffees and a pastry each. They had finished at the scene by the A9 and were on their way back into the station, but Hope had wanted to talk to her colleague. Despite being of junior rank, Ross was slightly older, and Hope saw him as a good listener when she needed to take stock.

Once Hope had installed herself back into the passenger seat, she distributed the food but watched Ross shift uncomfortably in the driver's seat. 'You okay?' she asked.

'Just my back playing up, sitting around too much I think or something. I don't know, maybe a bit of stress, it's a pretty grim one, this time.'

'True. I wanted to tell you that the boss is feeling it this time, believes he and his own may be under threat. So, he's asked me to keep a special lookout on what's happening, and if that goes for me, it goes for you. DC Stewart has her own issues after the attack she suffered in Newcastle so we'll not have this conversation with her. She needs to function as best she can, not think someone's after the boss or even us.'

Ross nodded and then shifted round to face Hope more. 'Tell me if I'm being a bit over the top but do you think there's someone on the inside here. There seems to be an awful lot of research to get the exact victims, to lay blame at the boss.'

'It's funny you say that,' said Hope,' but he also was of that opinion. But the pair of you do work by instinct more than Stewart or me. You seem to see the danger quicker.'

'Well, if he's of that opinion, I'd certainly take it seriously; it's what he's good at. He can't just simply acknowledge he feels uncomfortable with a gay man on his team, but he'll sniff out the most hidden vein in any investigation.'

Hope laughed. 'He's not particularly good with all the modern way of living, is he? But they say he's better than he was.'

'Don't get me wrong—he's never said anything against me or my lifestyle but he's just awkward around it. Guess it must be hard if you've been brought up to think it's wrong. But he has a nose and I'd back it any day.'

Hope supped on her coffee, more thinking than drinking. 'With that in mind, Alan, what do we have on the black Corsa?'

'We traced it down and Swansea has given us a photograph from the licence of a Dermott Vaughn. Bearded bloke with glasses and has a youthful look but I think there's something not right about the photograph, so I've sent it on to Jona Nakamura. I've also listed him to be on every constable's radar but there's been nothing so far.'

'What's wrong with the photograph?'

'The nose is wrong. At least it doesn't look normal. The beard kind of takes away from it but it looks inflated to my mind.'

'You're bothered he has a big nose?'

Ross laughed and then seemed to muse on something. 'Remember the Skye bridge bombing and the boss said the bomber might not be a woman because of how they jiggled.

Well, it's that kind of thing with the nose. Something is bothering me.'

Hope laughed. 'So, he has nostrils that are too big for the nose.'

Ross went deadly serious. 'That's it, but not too big. The nostrils are too small, like the rest of the nose has been built up around it. The flesh above the nostril is too thick to be normal. Hang on; I'm going to ring Jona.'

Hope sat back, a little surprised but eagerly anticipating a conversation about nostril sizes. Slowly chewing her coffee with every sip, Hope watched Ross get extremely animated as he fought to describe to Jona what was wrong with Dermott Vaughn's nose. His hands would form shapes Jona could never see and Hope watched his face become perplexed as Jona fought to understand. After five minutes, he hung up.

'She's going to check but I think I caught her at a bad moment.
'

'Why do you say that?' asked Hope. At the house that morning, Jona had seemed okay, her normal self even amidst these brutal killings.

'She sounded a little tearful, which I've never known. She was in the middle of prepping the body of Carmen Tate, so maybe that had something to do with it.'

Hope sat back in the seat and decided she would need to see if her housemate was really okay that night. The pressures of a case like this were rare and she would need to be aware of everyone working around her. Hope asked Ross to start driving back to the station and then saw a newspaper billboard with a headline EXECUTIONER SETS RIGHT SOFT JUSTICE. The papers would play up Carmen Tate's history of kidnapping and killing a child but the very public revelation of this would now start to cause a panic in the world of the convicted, especially those just released or who had served their sentences.

More than that, a certain section of the community would actually be okay with what was happening to the perpetrators of these previous crimes and others may withhold information because of fear of a killer's retribution. It seemed things would only get harder in the days to follow. But there were three dead already and Hope would have to make headway fast if there was not to be more victims of the Executioner. Dammit, that was one catchy name for the killer. It was going to stick.

Chapter 12

Hope stared at her wardrobe and the cream blouse hanging. It was a more professional look for the force, especially as a detective but she could not get away with the fact she was always at home in a pair of jeans and a t-shirt, or at least something in that laid-back ilk. Behind her a pair of crisp black trousers, ironed only that morning lay on the bed. If Jona had been here, she might have asked her, but she knew what Jona would have said. Wear what's comfortable. She knew Macleod was not bothered. In the past he might have been but after the senior members of the force deserting him during the supposed terrorist attacks around Fort William, he rarely mentioned it, in fact, had on occasion supported a more relaxed look for his team.

Hope took the trousers off the bed and hung them in her wardrobe, instead taking a pair of black jeans and a blue t-shirt and slipping them on. Yes, that felt better, and she found herself looking in the mirror. It was not something she did commonly, but she had found herself doing it more and more. Yes, she looked good, and tied her red hair up behind her in the ponytail she always wore when in work. But then she took another look in the mirror. Why was she still alone at night? How could someone like her who could catch the eye of men and women fail to be in a relationship at least?

Maybe it was a lack of a social circle. After all, who were her friends these days. There was Jona, housemate and a confident but also not interested in Hope in that way no matter how close they got as friends. Ross and Stewart, again neither of whom was a fit due to their preferences, not that Hope had any aspirations on either of her charges at work. Beyond that, there was Macleod, and he was attached. No, she thought, he was older, religious, grumpy, her boss and offended by what he saw as her free lifestyle. Or rather he had been. Now he was more protective of her, encouraging her in her career, telling her to wear the jeans and t-shirt, to be herself. There was something about him.

Hope shook her head as she heard the door of the house open. Stupid idea, girl, he's attached. Time for you to get back out on the dating scene. And for some reason, something inside felt extremely depressed about that thought.

'Just me,' shouted Jona up the stairs but Hope thought she sounded a little flat.

'You okay?' Hope asked remembering the conversation with Ross.

There was silence and Hope was about to go downstairs when she heard Jona's light footsteps come up the flight and the bedroom door opened. Jona tried a faint smile but it didn't work, and she half fell towards Hope. Catching her, Hope turned her to the bed where they both sat down, and Hope placed her arms around her.

'Hey, just a tough one.' She felt the sobs of Jona on her shoulder and simply held her. With a free hand, Hope ran her fingers through the Asian woman's hair and then across her shoulders. 'Easy.'

Jona lifted her face, eyes streaming tears. 'It's not right. We had to lift her down. No one should see that, have to do that. She was in such pain, her face so tight.'

It took Hope a half hour to get Jona into a shower and then tucked into bed. The alarm clock was set for four hours sleep and then Jona was wanting to return to the office. With the press now on the case, the higher echelons would be looking for results and Jona took her work very personally. So far there were few clues, which puzzled Hope. There was something almost professional about this killer and their attention to detail in not leaving any clues behind.

It was just past eight when Hope strode into the office and saw Ross behind his desk. The man was always there, arrived before her and departed after unless she shooed him home. His partner was often away, and it was a competition between them as to who could stay longest and avoid the empty house. Except that Jona's arrival meant that Hope usually had a friend waiting.

'Boss, I think I have something. It's actually come from Stewart, but she's gone home. She was still here at six when I got in—been on this all night.'

'So, what is it?' asked Hope.

'She checked CCTV of the areas of the killings,' said Ross. 'To be exact, she looked at the post offices where the packages containing Kyle McAvoy were posted. This was cross referenced with the road cameras near Marie Robert's house. There were not a lot of cameras close to the house, so Stewart had widened it out to main arteries heading that direction. She also grabbed images on the A9. They listed all the vehicles to see what they could match up. And there's one vehicle. A silver Berlingo.'

Hope nodded, impressed. 'A spacey ride, room to stick any number of things in there. The pole was sectional that Carmen Tate was hung on so they could have got that in a Berlingo. That's smart work by Kirsten. Listen Ross, let's keep this find to ourselves. I mean the team: the boss, Stewart, and us. The DI is worried that there might be someone on the inside and with how revealing this piece of information could be, let's keep it under wraps. But hunt down that car though.'

'Well, I have already got onto that side of things. I have the V5C form for ownership of the car, and it has an Alan Holmes as the owner and an address on the west side of Inverness. I checked up on that address and although it does exist, it's the ground of a local rugby team. I spoke to the chairman of the team this morning and there's no one at the club by that name. So, I looked at previous owners and the one before was a dealership. The car only changed hands a month ago. I'm on my way there this morning. They open at nine.'

'Excellent. Good work, Stewart and yourself. I'll brief the boss and then we are on the road.'

'It's not far,' said Ross, 'maybe ten minutes. No need to go for a while.'

'I need breakfast. You were right about Jona, Ross, had a bit of a falling apart this morning when she got in. Missed my toast so we're off to eat.' When Ross gave a protesting look, Hope simply waved him off and took out her mobile to call Macleod.

The car dealership was not one of those pristine forecourts off the main road in Inverness where all the dealerships seemed to hang out. This one was small forecourt near the docks behind a wire fence. There were maybe twenty cars on display, and they all seemed to be second hand. Not that Hope was in

102

any way a snob about her cars. In fact, she had only bought second hand.

As they approached the portacabin that presumably was operating as a main office, a woman approached dressed in heels and a tight if not short skirt. She wore a smart jacket and had maybe ten years on Hope, but she could certainly work her figure. Seeing Ross with Hope, the woman immediately made for him.

'Well now, I see a man who knows what he wants right there. You look like a man who can handle a real car.' Hope noticed that Ross was standing beside a Porsche and had suddenly become a little bemused by the woman's full on approach. 'If you want to take a seat inside, sir, I can furnish you with all the specifications about her.'

Reaching inside his jacket, Ross pulled out his warrant card and held it before the woman. 'Sorry to bother you but we are currently investigating a series of incidents where we believe a car bought here may have been involved. We need to check on the details of the buyer and also anyone who may have met them. Perhaps your office would be a better place to discuss this.'

Hope saw the woman look a little crestfallen, but she noted that the woman positioned herself between Ross and Hope as they made their way to the Portacabin. Once inside, the woman offered tea and coffee before introducing herself.

'Karen Macduff, at your service, hence Macduff Motors. How can I help you?'

Hope noticed the woman was addressing Ross and felt the need to put her right with who was in charge. 'I'm DS McGrath and my colleague is DC Ross. We're investigating the owner of a silver Berlingo purchased here about a month ago. We have the registration plate and have checked with the DVLA but have been unable to trace the driver. I need to know if you, or any staff, had dealings face to face with the gentleman and do they remember him?'

'Can you give me the car registration, please?'

Ross passed the letters and numbers and Hope watched Karen enter the details onto her computer. She sat back momentarily and then nodded her head. 'I thought as much. It wasn't me who sold that one—it was Ingrid. She's a student working for me part-time. Not the greatest with cars but she looks great standing on the forecourt. I mean you've seen some of the cars, they are for men who think with what's between their legs not their wallets, so you need a good-looking girl on the tarmac. Her English is not great, but I've seen guys nearly fall over themselves to buy a car from her.'

'Is she working today?' asked Hope.

'She should be here soon. She's doing a couple of hours for me.'

'I take it you have CCTV for the forecourt,' said Ross.

'I do, detective, but unfortunately, I think that recording has gone. It's there in case we get a theft, and we haven't had one, so the recording has probably been wiped. I'll check but I'm quite sure.'

Hope cursed internally and got to her feet, looking out the door of the portacabin for the arriving Ingrid. Part of Hope felt annoyed that a student had to come in and basically tease men, as it seemed demeaning. But it was not like men were making her do it. It was just another woman exploiting a fact of life. Well, Hope would not do it. As much as she liked being adored, she was no piece of meat to bring the wolves into the trap.

Ingrid arrived some ten minutes later and contrary to what Hope had expected she was not dressed in a smart skirt and blouse like her boss. Instead she wore a pair of casual trousers and a jumper, but Hope understood where Karen was coming from. Ingrid was a beauty, her long, blonde hair and tight-fitting clothes, coupled with a sweet innocent smile, would certainly bring any man over. Once she was inside the office, Ross began to ask questions.

'Do you remember the man who bought the silver Berlingo?'

'Yes. He was rather funny, made me laugh. He had a ridiculous beard and glasses. I remember he was like, how do you say, a clown? The funny people at the circus, I think. And his nose, it was not red, but it was strange.'

Hope cast a glance at Ross who raised his eyebrows. 'Do you think you could describe him to a sketch artist, and we could get a picture?'

'You want me to draw a picture?'

Hope stood up and stepped outside, taking her mobile phone and calling the station for a sketch artist to attend the car dealership. Behind her, she heard Ross trying to explain the process a sketch artist would follow but to little success gauging by Ingrid's replies.

It was almost lunch time when Hope and Ross re-entered the office and made straight for Macleod's room where he immediately invited them to sit at his side table. Hope dropped the sketch provided by the artist on his desk and Macleod picked it up immediately. Hope then dropped another drawing of the man but this time without the beard and glasses, and with a thinner nose.

Macleod paced the room with the drawings before placing the first back on the table. He then took the second drawing and stood looking out into the car park with it. Turning back, he asked Hope to call DCI Dalwhinnie and asked if she would come down to the office. It took the DCI almost fifteen minutes to appear and Macleod remained silent the whole time, simply looking out of the window. Ross would cast a glance at Hope, wondering whether he should interrupt but Hope shook her head. The boss was pondering on something. If he had something to say, he would say it.

DCI Dalwhinnie strode into the room dressed in trousers and blouse with a smart jacket over the top. Before she could say a word, Macleod had turned around and handed her the drawing he was holding. Hope watched the woman stare at the picture and then a realisation came across her face.

'Where did you get this?' asked Dalwhinnie.

'The team looked at all the cars on CCTV around the killings, cross-referencing number plates and managed to find one at all three killings, or at least within a reasonable window. They then traced the car via its V5C form to the dealership where it was bought. The girl who sold the car described him for our sketch artist. He was wearing glasses and had a beard, which the girl thought to be false. The nose was also thinned down a little as he may have been using a prosthetic. That's the resultant image.'

'It can't be, Macleod. The man's older now, much older. He wouldn't look like this. Do you think he's now got a beard and a larger nose? Surely a coincidence.'

'I doubt it.'

'Sir,' protested Hope, 'could you fill in the rest of us sat over here in the dark?'

'The image the DCI is looking at is a close match to a protestor we knew from an old case. Seamus Holt was his name and the estate he was living on had been terrorised by a child sex offender. There were a number of cases and Mr Holt was vehemently aggrieved that we were not doing our job.'

'But the killer is dead,' said Dalwhinnie. 'He died two years after he was incarcerated.'

'Exactly,' said Macleod, 'of natural causes. No justice, do you see.'

'But Holt's an old man; he couldn't do these things,' protested Dalwhinnie.

Macleod simply turned back to the window and stared out. 'When there's a will, there's a way!'

Chapter 13

With the sketched picture being only a possible image of the suspect, Macleod decided to send Hope out to find the last known residence of Seamus Holt and question the man. Meanwhile Macleod and Ross would circulate the description in case it was someone else and also to see if anyone had spotted the silver Berlingo around the time of the killings. Hope checked the electoral register and found a Seamus Holt living in Aviemore, the winter resort south of Inverness. Taking her car, Hope drove along the A9 road through the mountains to Aviemore.

The address was located away from the main road and on the far side of Aviemore and took Hope to a small estate populated with bungalows. The roads were neatly kept and the view of the countryside was breath-taking, as was Aviemore's location in general. There were still a good number of tourists in the area despite the later month of the year and Hope believed the skiing in the Cairngorms was beginning to operate. Finding the address, she approached a red door that was beside a large window looking out onto a small front garden.

Hope rapped the door which had no knocker, and then saw someone look out of the window trying to catch a glimpse at whoever was there. Rapping again with a more authoritative tone, Hope waited for the door to open. A chain was taken back and the door opened slightly. A grey-haired woman peered out and Hope could only see the top of her hair and a pair of narrow eyes.

'DS Hope McGrath, ma'am, can I have a word?'

'Bring that warrant card closer,' said the woman and she stared at it as Hope shoved it right up to the door's opening. The door then opened fully, and a Hope saw an older woman dressed in a plain skirt and slippers with a jumper on top.

'What do you want?' spat the woman and Hope peered behind her to see if there was any other movement inside.

'Would Seamus Holt be in?'

'Hardly, Seamus is dead. Been nearly two months now since I put him in the ground.'

'Dead,' said Hope in surprise. 'According to the electoral register, he still lives here.'

'Well, you don't update that until they send out the forms and that, do you? It's not like he's going to vote anymore. You don't believe me, love, do you, swanning up here in your jeans and tight top. Where did you see that look? Are you today's Miami Vice?'

'When was the funeral?' asked Hope, a little taken aback.

'I told you, two months ago. You can go to the graveyard; it's not far. But if you want to ask Seamus some questions, you'd better take a medium with you because he's dead. Smoked himself to the grave, lung cancer. So, go on, piss off, glamour cop. Sick of your lot.'

Hope watched the woman go to shut the door and placed her foot forward stopping it from closing. 'Why? Why are you sick of us?'

'Don't they do research anymore or just send you out with

a perm and a makeover. Dolly cops, is it? Just there to make up the numbers and for all that diversity bollocks. Bet they all enjoy having a gander at you in the morning.'

Hope could tell she was being baited and simply kept her foot in the door. 'Seamus was a protestor against some killings back in the day. Is that where your complaint is coming from?'

'Protestor? Our estate was in the hands of a killer, a child killer at that. We should have hung that guy. Stuck him on a pole like that other bitch. But no, your guys protected him, kept him from us, and he gets three meals a day and a nice quiet cell with television and all that. Snuffs it quietly. He never paid for what he did.'

'He was convicted and sentenced,' said Hope and then regretted saying it.

'And that was justice. We stood and told you all what he needed doing to him. That animal should have been gutted. Fat lot of use your lot were. Stop none of the attacks and then kept us from him. You can piss off, copper. Take your fancy clothes and body with you. Bloody Barbie cop!'

Hope breathed deeply. It was never a problem when a man dismissed her as tart in her job, there by acts of gratification and not by the hard work and slog she had put in during her time. But for a woman to do it was infuriating. These days it seemed to come from women more than men as well, the latter too scared they would be sanctioned or attacked for it.

'Whatever you think of me, ma'am, I still have a job to do. Now kindly look at this drawing and tell me if you recognise this man.'

Hope unfolded the sketch completed by the artist guided by Ingrid from the car sales forecourt and watched the woman stumble backwards. Hope stepped forward, reaching for her, but the woman batted her hand away and then snatched the drawing off her, studying it intently.

'Where did you get this?' shouted the woman.

'It's a sketch made of a man who bought a car recently. Do you recognise him?'

'Of course, I pissing recognise him. It's Seamus, it's my Seamus. But you didn't get this picture recently. This is an old drawing. Seamus hadn't looked like that for over twenty years. Look at him, he was young then. We lived in Glasgow then, not up here. He hasn't looked like this in years. What are you doing to me with this?' screamed the woman and threw the drawing at Hope.

'Did you and Seamus ever have any children?'

'What? No! I can't, but thanks for bringing that up as well. Insensitive bitch. Get out of my house; get the hell out of my house before I get a lawyer on you.'

Hope remained in the doorway and thought hard. If Seamus was dead and they had no kids, then was this a cousin or brother?

'Mrs Holt, did Seamus have a brother or a relative that looked like this?'

'No!' the woman screamed and swung the door hard catching Hope's foot. Fortunately, her boots were strong enough that she did not feel any pain and she leaned in again.

'Did Seamus ever play around?'

This time the door was closed with such a force that Hope stepped backwards and nearly stumbled down the doorstep. 'No, now sod off,' came the weeping voice of the woman inside.

Hope returned to the car and drove a street away before stopping to think. If the man in the drawing looked like Seamus but was too young to be him recently, and given that he was dead too, then it had to be a relative of some sort. Either that or he had a doppelganger walking around which was not uncommon. But the connection with Macleod was too much of a coincidence. First things first, thought Hope and looked for a cemetery in Aviemore on her mobile. The results came back that there were none and that most of the cemeteries were in fact about twenty to thirty miles away. But the woman had said it was only round the corner.

Hope decided a quick drive would help and she took the car through and out of the other side of Aviemore but no signs for a cemetery were forthcoming. This time Hope decided to stop for a coffee in one of the local supermarkets while she would ponder the conundrum. The last thing she wanted was to go back to the house again and face that woman. If they had indeed been protesters, then she might get herself into annoying legal complaints when all she wanted was to confirm the man was dead.

Supping her coffee, Hope searched online for churches in Aviemore and saw several. But one that interested her was a small church in Rothiemurchus, the village just south of Aviemore. It was an English church—that is Anglican—and Hope remembered that a lot of those had graveyards. Maybe that was an option. Certainly, the Anglican churches were often used for burials and weddings by those who had fallen out with the national Scottish churches. It was worth a look.

Driving down a hedge-lined road, Hope saw a small white chapel hiding amongst trees at the roadside. Parking up, Hope went to the red door of the building and knocked. Finding it open, she stepped inside and shouted for someone. There was no response and it occurred to her that the church would be open. It was an Anglican thing that the doors stayed open for anyone who wanted to come in and pray or use the building for quiet with God. Macleod would have approved but part of Hope felt nervous.

It was of course a stupid thought as she was on her own and there was no one else here except God. And then it struck her that maybe that was it. There was no one else to pretend to. She looked at the cross on a small table at the front of the church. Again, something felt nervous inside her.

'Okay, you win. I'm lonely, okay?' And with that she stepped outside amazed at herself. How had she felt more under pressure there than at any other place? Still, she thought, God's not going to want me, dressing like a Barbie cop! Hope laughed but she was still feeling uncomfortable and so decided to search the graveyard as quickly as she could.

It did not take long to spot the fresh grave in the churchyard, along from a large oak tree. There was a simple stone erected at the head of the grave bearing the inscription, BELOVED HUSBAND AND ACTIVIST, SEAMUS JAMES HOLT. Hope sought the noticeboard all churches have and found the name of the minister and a contact telephone number. In a conversation that lasted only two minutes, the minister confirmed that Seamus Holt had indeed died and was buried in the church, their first burial there in almost twenty years. It had been chosen so that his wife was at a close distance to him as she did not drive.

Hope returned to her car and began to drive back to Inverness. It seemed there was no one who fitted the bill as a descendant of Holt, or as a sibling. But then, Hope thought, that was based on what Mrs Holt knew. What if she didn't know everything?

Hope pulled the car over and rang Macleod. He was in a

meeting, but Hope insisted he remove himself for five minutes.

'What is it?' he asked.

'I've been to Aviemore and it's a dead end there. Holt has passed on, died of lung cancer two months ago. Confirmed that with his wife and the minister, and have also seen the grave. Mrs Holt says he has no siblings, and they have no kids, so it looks like a blank here except I was wondering, do you know if he had an illegitimate kid?'

She heard Macleod blow out a quick breath, letting his lips vibrate. 'Now you are asking, Hope. I haven't a clue. I doubt his wife would know as she was a heck of woman, bitter and ready for a fight so if he had fathered another child he would not have said and if she'd known she would have ditched him by my reckoning. What do you want to do? I assume there's something you want to do, as you're ringing me.'

'I want to go to Glasgow and see if he does have a child, sir. If he does, we need to trace that child.'

'Agreed but I'd rather have you here.' Hope was kept in silence and she could tell Macleod was thinking. 'Hope, given my suspicions regarding a possible leak, I believe you should go. If anyone asks, we'll say you are having women's issues.'

'Women's issues, bloody hell—what century, Seoras?'

'Okay, migraines, I don't know. But be quick. And if you do find a son, don't stop; pull that thread the whole way.'

'Aye, sir.' Hope cancelled the call and spun the car out of the lay-by turning it to drive south. It was midday and she could be in Glasgow by three if she drove well. But she'd need to know where to look. Hope was about to put a request into one of the constables on the case when she remembered Macleod's discretion. Pressing the hands-free option on the mobile, she called Stewart. After all, Stewart had been going through all of the cases so, surely she would have the detail on what happened.

'Hello? Boss, what's the crisis?'

'Kirsten, sorry to wake you. You weren't sleeping, were you?'

'Yes, I was. What?'

'I want the low down on a case Macleod was involved in. Names and details of everyone as I'm looking for a possible illegitimate son. It's come out of your car hunting. Case involving Seamus Holt, the protestor.'

'Two minutes. I need a coffee and then I'll get you everything. Where shall we meet? Station?'

'No,' said Hope. 'I'm driving to Glasgow, Kirsten, and you have about two to three hours to get me up to speed and give me a line of attack.'

'On it, standby.' Hope could almost hear the glasses being pushed up the nose.

Chapter 14

Stewart scanned the computer screen before her, taking in the detail between the words on the document. Police reports were always filled with code and not the kind you could breakdown by finding a source book. You needed to be in the profession to understand what was being said behind some of the standard phrases.

In his day, the boss must have been much more rigid as she could hear the disgust he felt behind the impassive description of crimes or actions by perpetrators, or prostitutes, or by more nefarious operators. She wondered if he ever preached at them. He didn't do that now, but he was keen to force out an observation on life from time to time.

Her other boss, DS McGrath, had left the phone line open so Stewart restrained herself from singing quietly as she was prone to do when no one was listening. McGrath had also been watching her more closely since she had revealed her love of comic books and of cosplay, dressing up as a favourite character. The particular character that had exposed this particular enjoyment of hers just happened to be one of the sexier outfits she had worn. Yes, Stewart was reserved in the main, a fighter by nature but when she had fun, she went for it. And she could rock that outfit better than her boss could any day.

That was probably a conceit, but Stewart did not care. Life was better than it had ever been despite the difficulties she was having with the area of physical confrontation in work. But she was a fighter, and she would rise up again. That was the mantra in the mixed martial arts gym she belonged to, and she believed in it. And besides, her brother was happy despite his own struggles with life, delighted with his new career, and he had not had a meltdown for some months. And here she was, the ferret of the team, technical whizz kid and learning it all at the sharp end.

A hand touched her shoulder, and she realised her other boss, DI Macleod was behind her. Smiling at him, she raised her eyes to question what he wanted. The man gave a gentle shake of the head and Stewart went back to her screen.

'The arrest seems very tasty,' Stewart said to her speaker-phone. 'The boss seems to have been at the thick of it.'

'Who's on there?' asked Macleod, suddenly aware that it was not just Stewart and himself present at the moment, albeit the other person was not in the room.

'DS McGrath, sir. On her way to Glasgow and she wanted to get some details off me about the case that involved Seamus Holt.'

Macleod waved at Stewart, indicating that she should leave her seat for him to take up. Plonking himself beside the speakerphone, Macleod got so close to it, Stewart thought he was going to eat the device.

'What do you need, McGrath, you have the actual source right here?'

The speaker phone sparked into life. 'I'm just looking for the feelings and occurrences around the arrest of the suspect in the

117

case Holt was involved in. Any rumours about his connections, which you said you had drawn a blank on.'

'True, I did, but it was a rough do. The killer, Adam Jarrow was holed up inside his house and we had to fight our way in to get to him. Holt was outside with a crowd and placards. It was like the whole community was out. We had a line of officers around the house and the boys were getting spat on and a few got injured from rocks being thrown. If we had not been there, they would have killed him. There were slogans like 'hang the nonce' and things like that. I had to walk in with some of the uniforms and retrieve Jarrow. We had a blanket over his head and got a van right up close to the house but as we brought him out some protestors came through and I actually tackled one. There were a few punches and a bit of rough and tumble, but we got him away.'

'I thought DCI Dalwhinnie was the arresting officer though,' queried Stewart.

'She was, but in those days with that sort of trouble, we didn't put a woman in the middle of it. Better job for the boys. But of course, times have changed. Women didn't fight like you do, Stewart, or like the Sergeant. I'm afraid these days I'm no longer the brawn in the outfit.'

With that, Macleod swept away to his office, shouting at the speaker that McGrath was to contact him the moment she knew anything. There was a pause on the speaker for about a minute and then Stewart heard a voice say, 'Is he gone?'

'Yes, he's in his office.'

'Okay, so have a look at the report and tell me what it really says.'

Stewart scanned the report again. 'Well, it seems that DCI Dalwhinnie did actually attend initially and was attacked when she tried to get the crowd to disperse. She was hit by a protestor and Macleod stepped in. There was a large scuffle and the boss managed to detain three different suspects as well as rescue Dalwhinnie. He's commended in the report.'

'He kept that quiet. What else?'

'It says at one point, Holt nearby got through the lines and that he was screaming and whipping up the crowd,' advised Stewart.

'Was there anyone with him? Anyone noted in particular?'

Several men, Frasier, McBurney, Davidson, and there's a woman named here, a Mrs Mary O'Neil. She was arrested by the boss for disturbance of the peace.'

'Really? Do we have an address for her?'

'Got one here.' Stewart passed the address. 'It is quite old though, but I guess it's a starting point. Why are you after her particularly?'

'Just a hunch, Stewart. I think Holt was playing away from home, but keep that within the team, and by that, I mean the four of us. Until I have something, no one knows I'm off doing this. The boss is worried we might have a leak after Ross and you were chasing that other car. It might have been a set up to get time to commit the pole murder. Certainly was a distraction. Thanks, Stewart, now get back to trawling the cases and seeing if there are potential victims we can warn.'

Stewart cancelled the call and for a moment wished it could have been her racing down the A9 to seek out the potential lover of Seamus Holt. But then her last confrontations in the field came at her again. She clutched the desk as she felt a sweat forming on her brow. The sessions were helping but she was far from cured. And the Fort Augustus incident had not helped.

* * *

Hope spun the car into the estate and realised that her task was about to get that much harder. The doors of most of the houses were boarded up and a few simply had no door. Following the street, she came to number 43, a small council house flat that sat at the bottom of two others in a block of six.

Exiting the car, Hope made sure she locked the door as she saw two youths watching it from a distance. At least she wasn't in her blouse and trousers. Instead she had her leather jacket on with her jeans and probably did not look like a police officer but rather someone simply in the wrong part of town.

The door of the flat she wanted was boarded and looking in at the window, Hope saw that the flat was not only empty but was also trashed. There were beer cans and liquor bottles all over the place and possibly stale vomit on the floor. As she turned back to her car, pondering her next move, she became aware that the two youths were coming closer and now that she had a proper sight of them, she believed they were more like two men in their mid-twenties.

Both men were wearing tracksuit bottoms and had a hoodie over their heads. Hope watched them approach and one moved behind her while the first came up to her, smiling.

'All right, love, what you doing out here? Looking for a little action.'

Hope did not have time for this. 'Move on; otherwise, I'll arrest you both for interfering with a police officer in the line of her duties. Beat it.'

'Oh, I'll interfere with you, love, be the time of your life. They'll hear you scream how good it was from here to Edinburgh.'

Hope watched the man produce a switchblade knife from his pocket and allow it to spring open. 'I am seriously a police officer and I will arrest you if you don't drop that knife to the ground and walk away from here right now. You have threatened an officer with sexual assault, and I will use force to restrain you.'

'Restrain me, love. I'll have you held by the hands and feet while I—'

Hope felt a hand touch her bottom and another slip around her waist reaching for her jean button. She did not hesitate and elbowed the man behind her in the head before grabbing his wrist and twisting it violently causing him to yell and fall to the ground. As she glanced back at the first man, she saw him reach for her, in an obvious groping manner and she lashed out a kick at his shin. He bent down, cursing her and she again violently pulled the wrist of the second man who began to cry. She then grabbed the first man by the hair and pulled him up, grabbing his arm up his back and bringing her mouth beside his ear.

'You ever go for a woman like that again and I will take that knife and make sure you can't do anything to another woman ever again. You'll sing soprano, friend, for the rest of your life. Understand?' Hope twisted the man's arm hard behind him and he cried out nodding his head profusely. 'Now piss off!' Hope kicked his backside and then chased the second man away.

Strictly, she should have arrested him but then people would have known she was in Glasgow. There would be an arrest to be made and a lot of paperwork and statements. This was a quick get in and out visit but she was sure the two men would not forget her. Certainly not a pleasant area to live in.

Her trip seemed to have been wasted but as she got back into the car, Hope saw a steeple poking out from above some more council houses. It was worth a go but it might be a shot in the dark. Driving round the streets where she saw a dealer passing out packets to a junkie, she made her way to the steeple which belonged to St Martha's Catholic Church. The building was small and Hope again locked her car before she walked to the adjoining building at the side of the church. She knocked on the door and it was answered by a large lady in a brown skirt.

'Hello, my name's DS McGrath. I was wondering would the priest be in?'

'Father Carmichael is taking his afternoon constitutional, I'm afraid. Can you come back?'

'I'm afraid not,' said Hope. 'I need to see the Father right now. It is urgent.' It was only urgent in the sense that Hope needed to get back up the road if this was a wild goose chase and she was not waiting around while someone was snoozing.

'Of course,' said the housekeeper. 'Give me a moment to see if he's available. You can wait in the hall over there.'

Hope stood in a bare hallway except for a hat stand which also contained an integrated umbrella rack. The hallway was chilly and she wondered if anyone was going to come when after five minutes no one had come back to her. Then she heard the stuttering steps, and on looking up, she saw a frail man in a black suit with a dog collar on the front.

'Apologies, my dear, but I am somewhat under the weather. Please, Officer, come into my vestry and we can talk.'

Hope followed the doddering steps of the priest and took the seat he offered her on the far side of a large wooden desk. On the wall was a crucifix and a picture of the Pope. There was no way Hope would have a picture of Macleod on her office wall and she found the practice almost amusing.

'Forgive the intrusion, Father, DS McGrath, looking for Mary O'Neil. She used to live round the corner but the flat is now boarded up. Would you know where she is now?'

The old man nodded and then stood and walked to the window of his office. He pointed out of it and Hope stood up to see where he was indicating. She could see the gravestones even if she could not make out much else through the frosted window.

'Five years now. Had a hard life, did Mary, but a good soul despite her flaws. She carried so many secrets.'

'Such as?'

The man looked shocked. 'They were told in the confessional, my dear. I cannot break the confessional bond between a priest and his parishioner.'

'Specifically, did she have a son?'

The man smiled. 'She had many sons.'

'How many?'

'Six. Six strapping lads. They all came through here; all had their first communions with us. It's only recently the place has become as bad as it has. Prior to that we had quite a community here.'

'You also had a rather traumatic incident regarding a child killer.'

Hope saw the man lean forward and bless himself. 'Is that what you are looking for? Some sort of dredging up of that horrid time.'

'I've only asked if Mrs O'Neil had a son and mentioned that the community had a rough time. Why do you assume I'm dredging up that case in such a raw fashion?'

'Because one of Mrs O'Neil's sons was attacked by that killer.

Young Simon was truly fortunate to be alive. A friend walked in on the killer performing the most horrendous act with Simon. The boy was of course traumatised, and he struggled ever after that. His mother wanted the killer destroyed as anyone would. She never truly got over it, but she worked hard with the lad. When he moved away, I think that was what finally got to her.'

'Why did he move?'

'To be nearer some of his kin. The trouble with being with someone through their trauma, my dear officer, is that you can then become a reminder of that trauma every day. No matter what she did, Simon never healed in any true sense. It was such a shame. She died two months after he left, of a broken heart, I'm sure of it. But then her other children had already left. And of course, her husband had left her a few years before.'

'Do you have an address for Simon?' asked Hope.

'No, I'm afraid not; he didn't really like the church in the end. Forgiveness was not his mantra. But I might have a photograph of him as a boy. A Sunday school picture from back in the day.' The priest hobbled off to a bureau and started shuffling through pictures in a drawer. Shortly he returned and placed a colour photograph before Hope.

'There, with his brothers.' Hope followed the finger to a group of six boys, five of whom looked similar, all with the identical haircut, a simple bowl. But the other lad who was younger had curly hair on top and a different smile. Hope's heart skipped a beat when she saw the face smiling out at her. She pulled the sketch that had been compiled and which she had shown to Mrs Holt, the one Mrs Holt had identified as her husband.

The face was a spitting image, younger and with hair on top

but in every way the eyes, nose and mouth looked so similar.

'I'm so sorry I could not be of more help to you, Officer,' the priest croaked.

'Oh, but you have Father. You really have.'

Chapter 15

Carl looked out of his bedroom window across the street to the five-bedroom house of Mrs Silvia Johnstone. It was of course a joint property, owned by Mrs Johnstone and her husband, whatever his name was. The building had an impressive balcony at its rear which looked out onto the green grass of the side of a small mountain, located just outside Inverness. The housing estate had been built very recently and there were no houses without at least four bedrooms, and all had an en suite—some had two. Carl believed that the Johnstone's house even had his and hers changing rooms off their main bedroom.

This was a detail he had noted from the brochures he had seen when his parents had bought the house. He liked the idea of Mrs Johnstone having her own changing room and, in his mind, she had an array of suitable nightwear simply hanging ready for whatever small slip she would be wearing that day. Like Carl, Mrs Johnstone would appreciate every detail of her house except for one thing that Carl hoped she had overlooked. In the design of the estate, the Johnstone's house was to be the star attraction but one which boasted a private anterior, a garden no one could see into and a balcony off the main bedroom that gave a stunning view of the countryside behind the estate. But little had the Johnstones believed that their more intimate moments on the balcony had been observed from the bedroom window of eighteen-year-old Carl Thomas.

Not that the moments had been particularly intimate, and Carl had frankly been disappointed how little Mr Johnstone had occupied Mrs Johnstone. It had been a quick cuddle or maybe tea together sitting in those glorious surroundings. But in Carl's mind that balcony and Mrs Johnstone were meant for somewhat steamier surroundings.

Carl had noticed that Silvia Johnstone had a fondness for staring at the stars at night. And if he were lucky, she would come out onto her balcony in her nightwear for a long lingering look at the clear sky while Mr Johnstone did whatever he deemed worth doing downstairs.

Tonight was no exception and the sky had been kind to Carl. There was barely any cloud and the stars shone bright as Silvia Johnstone stood with a glass of wine in her hand staring at the starlight. Her dressing gown was undone and Carl saw the woman of his dreams and found himself stuck to the view from his window.

But tonight, there was something different; for just for a moment, the lights in the Johnstone house had flickered. It was like the power had dropped in and out quickly on several occasions. At first Carl did not mind for it caused Silvia to step about on the balcony briefly and he always believed she looked better in motion than standing still. But then Carl believed he was dreaming as there seemed to be a haze around Silvia and she began to become more agitated. As long as she stayed on the balcony, Carl would not care. But then Carl saw a hint of orange from the bottom of the house.

Staring across, Carl saw the curtains in the window suddenly

127

go ablaze and his heart stopped. The house was on fire; Silvia was in trouble. Bolting from his bedroom, still in his boxer shorts and top, he knocked his father to one side as he descended the stairs. On the street outside, he ignored the small stones cutting into his feet and continued to run to the house whose front lay around another bend. As he reached the door, the bottom floor of the house was on fire and he heard windowpanes cracking.

Carl vaulted a low gate at the side of the house and began to shout out for Mrs Johnstone. The woman could be heard upstairs in hysterics.

'Mrs Johnstone! Silvia, I'm here, come to the edge. Have you got any sheets?'

Carl received no response and jumped onto a trellis that ran up the wall beside the balcony. Ignoring the fact that it was starting to pull away as he climbed, Carl reached the first-floor balcony and hauled himself onto it before scrambling into the Johnstone's bedroom. He saw Mrs Johnstone screaming as she opened the bedroom door and fire raced at her. As she turned from the flames, Silvia stared in disbelief at the boy in boxer shorts staring back at her.

'We need to get out, Silvia,' shouted Carl but the woman stood still staring at him. Carl peered over the balcony and saw the trellis had fallen away. 'Are the stairs usable? Silvia, I'm going to save you. Are the stairs okay?'

When the woman did not flinch, frozen in shock, Carl ran to the bedroom door and opened it. The stairs seemed to be on fire. But the more he stared, Carl realised than it was the furnishings around the stairs that were burning, not the stair carpet yet. He turned and grabbed Silvia Johnstone by the hand.

Carl had to pull the frightened woman harder than he realised he would need to, but he managed to get her feet moving and take her down the stairs. The front door was blistering but had not yet caught fire. Carl turned the door handle and screamed as he felt a searing heat go to his fingers. But the door opened and he was ready to drag Silvia to the safe air beyond.

Silvia had seen her husband in the front room and was now flailing towards him. Carl followed and then stopped in horror as he saw a man who was motionless but who clearly had burn marks across him but not from the fire. The chair he sat in was an oasis in the burning lounge and was about to ignite, but the man clearly had been burnt in parts.

Then part of the roof fell down across the lounge beyond them. Carl grabbed Mrs Johnstone and dragged her with all his strength out of the front door. Standing in the front garden were his parents and a number of other neighbours, screaming and shouting. He pulled Silvia away as she tried to turn back to the house. Her husband was clearly dead. Carl held the woman and she suddenly clung to him, weeping bitterly into his shoulder.

Despite the heat from the house and the excited neighbours around him, Carl somehow felt good with what was happening.

* * *

Macleod stumbled into the car and looked across at Stewart. 'Why am I going to a burnt house at two in the morning?'

'Morning, sir. There's been an incident just north of Inverness and we've been asked to attend. I'm not sure why

129

but the scenes of crime took one look at the place and called Jona Nakamura who asked for our attendance. Jona's on her way as well.'

'She asked for us before she had even seen the place?'

'That's correct, sir. I'm sorry but I was unable to stop for coffee on the way. Macleod reached behind his seat and showed a flask to Stewart. 'The joy of having a good woman in your life. She made it before I was even dressed.'

'Was she not sleeping?'

'No Stewart, she was not. She still has flashbacks from the bus accident. We rarely get a full night's sleep.'

'Sorry to hear that, sir.'

'Not as sorry as me, Stewart. Still, job to do—let's go.'

The pair arrived at the new estate and Macleod saw the array of fire engines, police vehicles, and ambulances as well as the scene of crime officers. It looked like the ambulances were departing but Macleod could see the Fire Chief with his distinct tabard and made a direct line for him. Beside him stood a police Sergeant in uniform who nodded at Macleod as he approached. Macleod extended a hand to both men and announced himself.

'What was the cause, Chief?' asked Macleod.

'It appears that the electrics were under a massive power surge but the fuse box did not trip and the energy caused a fire to break out on the downstairs circuit. At least that's the hypothesis. I think there's going to need to be a much more detailed examination required before we know exactly. But there is one fly in the ointment. If you'll see your forensic people. I've just declared the fire as extinguished, but the house structure is unsafe. So, follow the instructions of your forensic teams. They know where is safe and where isn't.'

Macleod thanked the man and headed straight for Jona Nakamura, the diminutive Asian woman who was standing beside two forensic officers and debating something.

'Miss Nakamura, as much as I delight in seeing your charming persona, why am I here at this ridiculous hour of the morning?'

'Inspector, I'm glad you could make it. This is a strange one and I was just discussing how much electricity is required to make an electric chair. Also, where do you need to tap into a circuit to boost the charge?'

'An electric chair?' Macleod shook his head as if trying to knock out some sort of dirt from his eyes.

'Yes, sir. Come with me but please suit up first.'

It took Macleod two minutes to don the white coverall suit and boots and follow Jona into the house and to the lounge area. He fought to control his stomach at the sight before him. The eyes of a man protruded from their sockets and there was a contortion in the face that was not normal. There also seemed to be several burns across the body, at least that which was not burnt black from fire.

'Jona, what on earth?'

'Electric chair, at least a pretty ropey one. The current used was oversized and the man was probably dead almost instantaneously. I'm still trying to see exactly how it was done but someone was here in the house and made the final connections. We think they came from the grid but it's too early to tell. This is mainly guesswork, Inspector, but however they did it exactly, they used an electric chair of sorts. This could be our killer again.'

Macleod shook his head and walked away. Returning outside, he saw Stewart. 'Stewart, find me who I need to see

131

and talk to and then come get me. I need a bit of air.' Macleod lowered his voice. 'There's a damn electric chair in there.'

The world seemed to swim for a moment and maybe it was the early hours of the morning doing it to him but for maybe only the second time in his career, Macleod felt himself physically affected by a death. The smell of the body was not what was causing this. The first time it had happened he was a first-year officer and a first dead body causing shock was normal. But now after seeing his fair share of deceased parties, he was taken aback by how his body was struggling with this one.

The lights of the police cars were somewhat blinding and Macleod felt disorientated. Leaning up against a police car, he had a sudden chill run down his back. What if this had been the plan for his house? There had been someone spying on it. Maybe it had been the press, but in his heart, he knew it was something more sinister. What if the chair had been for him? Moreover, what if it had been for Jane? Macleod had never had so much to lose since the death of his wife, Hope. And now after seeing Jane surviving a bus accident, and just when he felt they were turning a corner in her recovery, Macleod realised he was not in control.

It was not an uncommon feeling to not be fully in control of a murder investigation, but usually you and your kin were not on the list of the potential victims. Even back on the Isle of Harris when he had been trapped with Hope in the estate house, fighting to uncover the plot that had threatened their lives, he had not felt like this. And they had so few leads. Everything was coming up empty. And there was a potential mole. Macleod did not mind if others did not believe him, never had a problem with not being supported, but now he felt a grip from an unknown assailant, but one who obviously knew him from the past and was very much in his future.

Stewart tapped him on the shoulder and Macleod fought to bring himself round and try to look as professional as possible. But on this cold night, he could feel the sweat on his brow from the terror that was building inside. Some people said that the greatest terror was seeing something so shocking that it made you sick or shut down completely. Macleod disagreed. This was true terror, that building fear that you cannot keep safe those around you, and in particular, the one you love.

None of these things were evident to Silvia Johnstone sitting in the rear of an ambulance as she was joined by Macleod and Stewart. Beside Silvia, Carl was holding her hand like a faithful Labrador. Macleod was unsure if the woman was even aware her hand was being held. The paramedic had briefed them that she was in shock and that they may not get anything of substance from her and that they should treat anything she said with caution.

'Mrs Johnstone, I'm DI Macleod, investigating your husband's death and the fire at your house. I need you to focus for a bit, to try and answer some questions.'

The woman's face was pale and she did not seem to even register Macleod's presence. He glanced at Stewart who, every ready, pushed her glasses up her nose and leant in close to the woman.

'Silvia Johnstone, my name's DC Stewart but you can call me Kirsten. We need to ask you some things. Is that okay? Mrs Johnstone, I asked if that was okay.' The woman barely nodded so Stewart continued. 'Were you out this evening?'

The woman nodded. 'Out. Yes, we were out.'

'Where?'

The woman looked out of the ambulance as if the answer was simply floating past. 'Theatre.'

'What did you go to see?' asked Stewart. She watched Mrs Johnstone start to say something several times but then she just stopped and stared blankly ahead. As Stewart traced her gaze, she saw it was inside the ambulance, looking at a pack on the wall. That's where her eyes were but who knew where the mind was. 'When you came home, was there anyone about?'

Again, there was nothing and Macleod stepped out of the ambulance hailing the paramedic. 'I don't think we should delay you any further. She's saying nothing. Best she gets to hospital and we'll drop by tomorrow and see if she's in a better state. The paramedic nodded and she shouted to her colleague who jumped into the rear of the ambulance. Stewart stepped out but when the paramedic asked Carl to leave, he clung on to Mrs Johnstone.

'Are you family, sir?' asked the paramedic.

'Not yet,' answered the teenager. Macleod clocked his head at this and walked into the back of the ambulance taking Carl by the arm.

'We need to speak to you. I think you should let Mrs Johnstone get to hospital and get some rest. You can visit her tomorrow after she's rested, I'm sure. For now, we require your assistance.' Macleod became aware that the young man was in boxer shorts and bare feet. Gently, he led the man out and shouted at Stewart to get a thermal blanket. She appeared with a silver foil cover from somewhere and wrapped it around the young man.

'Do you live here,' Macleod glanced at Stewart who mouthed a word, 'Carl?'

'Just around the corner.'

'So how did you end up here rescuing Mrs Johnstone in your boxer shorts and a top? Seems a bit scant for a rescue mission.'

'I saw the house on fire so I ran to help.' The man looked somewhat twitchy and Macleod wondered if he was hiding something. The Inspector remembered the man's response to the question of family—*Not yet.*

'Were you watching Mrs Johnstone?'

Carl looked up at Macleod and managed a smile. 'Who wouldn't, sir? She is magnificent? Was looking at her from my bedroom window as she stood on her balcony looking at the stars. She's a sensitive woman, not some airhead. Cultured, always out and about. And simply fantastic in her . . .'

Carl ran to a halt and blushed. So, he had seen her in private clothing, thought Macleod. A peeping Tom. 'And did you see the fire start?'

'There was a power flicker of sorts and then as Silvia was on the balcony, I saw fire below. She was unaware of it, so I ran to save her.'

'In your bare feet and boxer shorts?'

'She was at risk, I needed to save her. She hugged me afterwards; she knew she was safe in my arms.'

Macleod shot a glance at Stewart who raised her eyebrows. 'Okay, and did you see Mr Johnstone during this whole time?'

'Only when she ran in to try and save him,' said Carl. 'But he's dead. His body was burnt. Was pretty horrible. But she was not interested in him really, just being a decent person trying to save him.'

'Why do you say she was not interested in him? They had been out at the theatre and she seems pretty distraught.'

'She's just in shock at how it happened. Silvia was up on the balcony for me. I think she knew I looked. She never looked back so I wouldn't know she knew but she smiled a lot. She enjoyed me watching.'

Macleod called over a uniformed officer and asked him to take down Carl's details and then to find his home and his parents. Macleod suspected they were the two people watching at the edge of the police line.

'Dirty little pervert,' said Stewart when Carl was gone.

'Hormones, Stewart, affects the male different to the female. A crush on an older woman is nothing unusual. But he does have it bad.'

'Delusional, I'd say. You don't think there's any chance he could be involved?'

Macleod shook his head. 'Mr Johnstone's past is where you'll find the answer to why he's in that chair. But this took time to set up. Yes, the Johnstones were out so who was here?' Macleod took a look around him and saw the next house along was brightly lit up with a man standing in the driveway. On the other side, the house was in the dark.

'Stewart, has anyone been to that house?'

'Yes, sir, but no answer. Believed they are away.'

'Really, there's a car in the drive. Where's the officer who went over? Find him for me, please and ask him to join me there.'

It was five minutes later that a thick-set constable stood beside Macleod at the front door as the Inspector rang the doorbell. No one came and no lights were lit.

'That's exactly what happened with me, sir. I did try and look in the front window but there was nothing.'

'What about the car?' asked Macleod.

'Neighbour said they have two. Might be away.'

'Might is not good enough, constable. They are right next

door and potential witnesses to what may have occurred so let's make sure what you think is accurate. Let's go round the back. When you say there was nothing in the front window, how do you mean that?'

'I could not see through the blinds, sir.'

The officer followed Macleod round the house with Stewart in tow at the rear. On reaching the rear, Macleod saw a large window which was in line with the obscured window at the front. But here the curtains were open, and he looked inside.

A family were sitting on a sofa facing Macleod and he saw the shape of a gun on a tripod pointing at them. The father saw Macleod and started screaming at him. 'No, he'll shoot us; he'll shoot us.'

'Break the door,' Macleod shouted at the constable accompanying him and the man ran to the back door and threw his shoulder at it. The door remained firm. Macleod stared through the window where the whole family were agitated but clearly unable to get off the sofa. The constable continued to attack the door but he was having no success. Macleod began looking in the garden for something to throw when Stewart tore past him with something in her hands. Arriving at the back door she shouted at the constable to get clear and Macleod watched her hit the door with a handheld battering ram which broke the lock and caused the door to swing open.

Stewart dropped the item and raced into the house followed by Macleod. In his mind he was looking for a shooter, someone with a gun and when he entered the large through-lounge, he could only see the family on the sofa in the dark. There were five of them including two younger children. The father and mother were shouting now and trying to force the kids to lie down and Macleod watched Stewart knock the gun pointing

137

at the family to one side.

A light flooded the room and Macleod realised the constable behind them had switched on the main light for the room. Looking towards the rear window, Macleod saw a camera and stood in front of it before taking his coat and covering it. The father was still screaming.

'He said he'd kill us if we said anything, said he was watching us on the camera. Macleod scanned the room and could not see any other threat. 'Stewart, let's get these people out of here.' The Inspector glanced at the distraught husband and again thought of Jane. Macleod was at his limit with this killer.

Chapter 16

Macleod stared at the black liquid before him and watched the steam rising from it. He was exhausted but to go home and simply catch an hour's sleep was pointless. Instead, he had come into the station and grabbed a shower in the changing rooms before putting on a spare shirt he had in his locker for emergencies. Currently he had not put his tie back on as he was unlikely to see anyone of note until at least nine o'clock.

At times like these, he envied the younger officers he worked with. He had left Jona Nakamura at six in the morning and she looked remarkably well considering she had been up as long as he had. In fact, she was probably getting even less sleep than himself given she had been out at the site of the pole killing.

Macleod called Hope from his mobile, wondering if she would pick up at this early hour, but he discovered she was already in her car returning north.

'I stopped in a Travelodge last night and set off as soon as I woke up. I may have something, but it wouldn't hold up in court without a bit more. It's just a hunch, Seoras, but I do think Holt had a child and that child was abused by the killer in that case. He's the son of a Mrs O'Neil and he's the spitting image of Holt. Although that is a photograph of him as a child so I might just be seeing what I want.'

'Doesn't matter,' said Macleod, 'keep going on it. I've got an electrocuted man on my hands now. Our killer is getting more inventive although this time I think he may have stretched himself beyond his understanding.'

'Electrocuted?'

'Yes, on his sofa. It was like a home execution. But he, and we know it was a 'he' from the family he held captive next door, didn't fully understand his electrics because he put the house on fire. Jona's taking a look at it with some real experts. I'm going to look at the deceased with Stewart. Ross got to stay in bed last night so I had at least one of us who looked fresh this morning. But he's still chasing cars. We need something concrete to chase, Hope—feels like it's always shadows.'

'Isn't it always, sir?' queried Hope.

'Yes, but normally our families are not involved. There's something inside me that knows he's coming for me in some way. It makes sense that his full fury has to focus somewhere.'

Hope yawned. 'Sorry Seoras, but it seems his full fury is on the poor sods who end up dying. It's not like he simply dispatches them; there's no mercy.'

'Keep at it; I'll keep you covered from this end.'

'But Seoras, surely I'm now running a proper lead, you need to keep Dalwhinnie and company in the loop?'

Macleod blinked trying to stop his eyes from blurring as he looked at his desk before him. 'No. Not until I work out if we have a mole. He's been ahead of us, set up decoys that have yanked us here and there. We work in secret only letting out what we want to let out or what is obvious from other sources. He needs to be unaware that you are on to him.'

'Am I?'

'You're closer than any of us, so keep going. Mobiles only for contact or a face to face.'

'Has anyone asked for me?' enquired Hope.

'Dalwhinnie did mention you in passing.'

'What did you say?'

'Woman's things. She looked at me as if I didn't have a clue. I told you it was good cover.' Macleod made a half laugh but he was having to force it.

'Seoras,' laughed Hope, 'I'll be in touch.'

Macleod went back to staring at his coffee cup which was steaming less than before. His mind was foggy, like someone had a screen and kept passing it before his eyes so he could not see the full picture. But it was there; he would just have to dig. A knock on his office door snapped him back to the moment and he called Stewart in. She had not been home either but for some reason there was little evidence of this.

Normally Stewart wore a pair of black trousers, a white blouse, and a black jacket but at this moment she had a pair of jeans and a t-shirt with a mixed martial arts logo on it. Obviously, she was feeling self-conscious about this as she was wearing her outside jacket, a kind of baseball jacket.

'Apologies for the look, sir,' Stewart said as she came before Macleod's desk, 'but I don't have any spare workwear here, just what I wear down to the gym after work. I'll change as soon as I can.'

Stewart looked closer to McGrath than her normal self, but Macleod thought the look suited her. He had rarely seen her outside of work and often struggled to imagine her in an MMA ring. 'Don't bother yourself, Kirsten, you look great. I wish I could still wear younger clothing. I'm more of a cardigan man these days.' Stewart smiled and Macleod found himself in one of few moments when he might have read the opposite sex correctly.

'I've been going through the details on our victim from last night, sir. Paul Silas Johnstone, American citizen, or at least he was. His status is unsure due to botched extradition proceedings. The man was a lawyer for some American gangsters. One of their number had caused trouble over here with some working girls, killed a few of them. Mr Johnstone was also believed to have killed over in America to help cover this up and although he represented the gangster, Mr Johnstone was also wanted by the Americans for the killing over there. Long story short, the extradition was cocked up big time. But you helped take the man into custody in front of another angry mob. Although this time it seems less of a lynching attempt. I think our killer might be struggling for victims that fit the criteria.'

'Well it's good to know my entire career has not been simply about rescuing killers from the hands of the public, Stewart. I want you to work out what files needed to be accessed to know this information and then find out who accessed those files recently. Keep it quiet that you are doing it and if you need any help, let me know and I'll sign off what you need.'

Stewart nodded and went to stand but then stopped. 'Jona Nakamura called. The whole setup at the neighbours was false. The weapon pointed at the family, the cameras, all replicas, nothing was genuine. He played them.'

'How did he get them into that position?'

'Called as a council inspector, looking at drains. The wife let him in, and he pulled a gun on her. Threatened to kill her and managed to get the family into one room where he injected them to knock them out. When they came to, he had tied them

142

to the sofa, and he gave them all the nonsense about he was watching and ready to kill them at any time. Very elaborate but really not requiring a lot of equipment. Looks like he was able to get at the electricity supply from there and also into the Johnstone's house. No one saw anything untoward as he simply took the other car away making people think the family had gone out.'

Macleod stood up. 'He's getting braver, Stewart.'

'That's not a good thing, sir.'

'No, it's not but it might mean he makes his real play, goes for what this is all about. Get into those files and see who's been looking. We need to get on top of this quick.' Macleod had not said but he thought the final play would be about him, or someone close to him.

'Oh, sir?'

'Yes, Stewart.'

'No card at the crime scene. Nothing with your name on it. Looks like the fire might have burnt it.'

'How well known is this?'

Stewart shook her shoulders but then offered, 'Well, the Sergeant at the scene knew, forensics, upstairs too, as Jona will report that as a difference between scenes.'

'Do you gamble, Stewart?'

'Occasionally, sir, odd Grand National bet. Why?'

Macleod grinned. 'What's the odds on the next post having a card in it?'

'Unlikely, sir. The cards have all been placed at the scene.' Stewart frowned, not seeing Macleod's point.

'Don't gamble, Stewart, you'll lose. Next post will have a card and it will be franked too, with yesterday's date.'

'How do you know that, sir?'

'The mole, Stewart. I'll explain when it comes.'

Stewart departed and Macleod clenched his fist. He was angry because he was beginning to suspect the killer was from inside the force, and right here in the Inverness station.

Macleod called home that morning to check if everything was all right and got a clean bill of health from Jane. She had been walking in their garden and was feeling better physically. However, she mentioned the person who had been spying on their house six times in the half hour conversation saying each time she was not worried. Macleod understood she was beginning to stress about it. He was used to the pressure and he was struggling to not panic.

Mackintosh, when he spoke to her, was much more circumspect. There had been no more incidents, the police car was still outside, and the men were patrolling every half hour around the house. Mackintosh was also keeping all the doors locked whenever they were inside the house. Hazel was going into work mode, like Macleod was, doing what had to be done until the crisis was over. Only then would they fall apart and pay back the bill the stress was running up.

At two o'clock, Stewart walked into Macleod's office and threw a small envelope down on the desk. There was a first-class stamp on the top right corner, and it was franked with yesterday's date. The card was addressed to Macleod and he took a pair of gloves from his desk before using a letter opener to cut the top apart.

Finding a card inside, he took it out and saw his name on one side. On the reverse were some simple words in large capital letters. THIS IS HOW TO DEAL WITH PIRATES.

Chapter 17

The journey up from Glasgow had been strenuous despite the fact she was only driving for around four hours. Hope had slept somewhat fitfully the night before and was pondering on the fact that Macleod believed she was closer to catching the killer than anyone else. There was a degree of pressure in that, especially as the body count was mounting. Macleod was seeming quite calm, but Hope believed that was simply a false exterior and that inside he was scared by the man who had been seen at his home. Jane had become her boss's world. Everything outside of the job was with Jane. He had no other hobbies—just her and whatever she did.

There was something about devotion like that which stirred sentimental feelings about Macleod, feelings she quickly squashed. It was funny how working together had brought them closer and she understood him so much better than that first case on Lewis. There was deepness to the man which had thrived when he had learnt to throw off the regret over his wife's death. And Jane had then taken that step of Macleod's and taught him to run again. The bus accident had nearly crushed him, and now this.

Hope's investigations had given her an address for Simon

O'Neil, Mrs O'Neil's son whose father was Seamus Holt. There had been driving licence records which had taken Hope most of the evening to acquire and they gave an address in Inverness. The exact location was on the road out to Beauly to the west of Inverness and then a small track to an old farmhouse. The DVLA said that the address had been changed some five years ago and that Simon O'Neil had no endorsements attached to the licence. But then the correlation between driving offences and a desire to murder was never proven.

Hope finished off the remnants of her chicken sandwich she had bought from a petrol station on her way up from Glasgow and drank her orange juice, before stepping from the car and approaching the door of the farmhouse.

The building looked as if it might have two or three rooms and an attic. A small chimney emerged from the roof towards the rear and Hope wondered what the interior décor was like. She could not see through the frosted glass that half-filled the front door and she decided to take a walk around the rear of the building when her knocking gave no response.

From the rear, Hope was able to look into the kitchen and saw a basic wooden table with a couple of chairs. There was an AGA stove, and she clocked the small wood pile near the back door. There was no life in the house and the rear door, like the front, was locked. Returning to the front, Hope heard a tractor nearby and turned to see a large red one making its way down the drive she had recently come down.

'Hello, there,' shouted a man from inside the tractor as it arrived, and Hope stared up at the vehicle. It was not a quaint old tractor but rather a modern one and towered over Hope. The man jumped down from the cab and stood in his boiler suit and wellington boots, giving her a friendly smile.

'Are you looking for Simon?' asked the man.

'Yes,' said Hope. 'I'm DS McGrath and I'd like to speak to Mr O'Neil.'

'What about?' asked the man, still smiling.

'I'm sorry, sir, but that's between Mr O'Neil and myself. Can I ask your name and how you know Mr O'Neil?'

The man did not lose his joviality and reached forward with a mucky hand. 'David Bairstow, delighted to meet you. I own this house and most of the land you can see. I rented this little place out a number of years ago and Simon has been my one and only tenant. Is he in trouble?'

'I hope not,' said McGrath, in a response she had learned from Macleod. It was friendly but gave away absolutely nothing about whether you were hunting the individual or concerned for their safety. 'Do you know where he is?'

'I'm afraid not. He owes me his rent but sometimes he disappears for a while and then comes back. He's never not paid and usually on time. Likes to keep himself to himself. Pleasant enough but it's certainly his space now he's rented it. Which is correct of course but he's very private.'

'When did you last see him?'

'Oh, let me see,' pondered David Bairstow. 'Been at least a month. He gave no indication he was disappearing off but then again, he never does. He has no pets or friends as far as I am aware. But never a hassle and certainly friendly enough when we do talk.'

'Do you know if he attends any clubs or groups?'

'Well, it's funny you should say that as that's why I came down in the tractor. Saw your car and wondered if he had a friend coming. To be honest, when I saw you, I thought, oh aye, he's got himself a woman and I fancied seeing who she was. It was the red hair, love. My Dawn's got red hair too, and I honestly adore it. Sorry, a bit forward, not meaning anything by that.'

Hope smiled at the man who she found rather endearing. However, as an informant he was not a lot of use. 'So, no clubs or hobbies?'

'Well he did attend a victim's group, although I don't know what for. Friend of mine needed a lift home one night and I offered as his wife was elsewhere. Well, I'm in the car park and out comes my mate with Simon beside him. Simon didn't look too pleased to have me there. I never asked what it was all about because you're not meant to, are you? People's personal lives and all that.'

Hope swore internally at the man's lack of curiosity. 'What about your friend; what happened to him?'

'I don't like to say, and I hope you don't mind me not giving his name, but it was child abuse. All I know is it really helped him. I didn't ask my friend about Simon's particular case and it might not even be about that.'

'Do you know who leads the group?'

'Sure, it'll be on the church hall notice board, just back down the road towards Inverness. Inchmore Church.'

'Thank you, sir. Are you about today—I mean not disappearing off anywhere in case we need you to come and unlock the house for us?'

'Blimey. What's he done?'

'Nothing that I'm aware of, sir; it's routine in case we can't find him. In case he's in there and needing help, that sort of thing.'

'Ah, right, with you now, officer. Yes, I'm about. Our house is just over there and if I'm out on the tractor or that, Dawn will be in. As I said, red hair like yourself.'

Hope got into her car and made her way back towards Inverness but spotted Inchmore Church shortly afterwards. The grey building had a small car park and Hope spotted the noticeboard near the front door of the church. There was a list of groups and she struggled to see any that were directly about survivors of abuse. But there was one she could not identify, the CARE group and she noted the number of a Linda Flowers, the contact name for the group.

Calling the number from her mobile, Hope discovered that Miss Flowers worked in Inverness but agreed to meet Hope during her lunch hour on the shores of the Moray firth at the Merkinch Nature Reserve car park. Hope was ten minutes early arriving for their appointment and stood watching the Firth, chancing her arm that she might see a dolphin or two. In truth, after the long drive of the morning she drifted away somewhat and was brought back to earth by the sound of a woman's voice.

'Is that you, Officer? Linda Flowers here. I could tell by your red hair, very distinctive.' Hope turned around and saw a young blonde woman dressed in a fleece and a pair of jeans.

'DS McGrath, Miss Flowers; thank you for coming.' Hope extended a hand and Linda shook it. 'I need to ask you some questions about a Simon O'Neil who I believe comes to your group.'

'I'm afraid most of what we discuss is confidential. I'm not sure how much I can help you.'

'And there's a lot I cannot tell you,' said Hope, 'but be advised that I am investigating some serious crimes and that I need to know the whereabouts of Simon.'

'For his protection?'

Hope thought about this. Well, Macleod was often protecting the arrested, as this case was showing so she did not have to lie. 'Possibly. When did you see him last?'

'It was over a month ago, detective, at the group. In truth, that's the only place I think I have ever seen Simon. Always struck me as quite reclusive.'

'Did he have a job?'

'I believe so, at the library as I recall. The main one in Inverness, although I think he may have given that up. Just something he said. I couldn't work out if he had or if he had not, but I had a feeling. We're a very non-probing group, everyone at their own pace.'

'And what sort of a group is it exactly?' asked Hope.

Linda seemed to puff herself up with pride and smile before answering. 'We are CARE, Conversations about Abuse Recovery and Existence. I know it's a naff title, but I really wanted it to fit CARE.'

'So, it's safe to say Simon suffered abuse at some point in his life and needed to talk about it.'

Linda nodded. 'That's true but he was one of the more difficult people in the group. Simon was not good at moving on, constantly returning to the issue and looking at himself. I'm a volunteer and although I have some counselling skills, I am no expert. The group is merely a supportive forum. I don't think I can really say more about him without breaking confidence.'

'I may need to break into that confidence,' said Hope, 'but I will tell you why. However, for now that's plenty. By the way do you have a photograph of him?'

'No,' said Linda, 'there's no way we would take a photo of a confidential group.'

'I appreciate that,' said a frustrated Hope, 'but maybe you can describe him for me.'

'Thin hair, really; maybe five feet ten, something like that. Sorry, I know more of what he's like. I'm no good at describing people.'

'Maybe the library will have something,' said Hope. 'Thanks for your time and I have your number if we need to seek further from you, Miss Flowers.'

As Hope watched the woman depart, she wondered if there was something in this or was she simply chasing a disturbed man? Hope decided that she needed to update Macleod on what she had discovered and placed a call to his mobile. The call went straight to his voicemail and Hope closed it and called the station direct to find out where her boss was. This time there was no answer from the office and Hope was directed back to the switchboard.

Wondering what was afoot, she asked for the forensics laboratory, hoping to speak to Jona. Instead she got a male voice on the end of the line and one she did not recognise.

'Hello, Sergeant. I'm afraid that they have all gone to an incident that's taking place at the marina in Inverness. It seems there's another body been found. I'm not too sure of the details.'

'That explains why the DI's mobile is going straight to voicemail; he must be on the hoof. Not to worry but I'll get him soon enough.'

'Forgive me, Detective, but I was wondering why you weren't with him when they left.'

'Sometimes we have to spread the net wide,' replied Hope. 'Thanks for your help. Who is this anyway?'

'Cunningham, miss, Elijah Cunningham.'

Hope cancelled the call and tried to recollect who Elijah Cunningham was. Jona had many colleagues working in forensics and Hope could not remember all of them but she usually had a face to hold the name up to. But this name was giving nothing away.

Looking out at the Firth, Hope pondered what she should do. There was another body but Macleod was onto that. If he wanted her assistance he would call, and Macleod had basically told her if anyone was going to get to the bottom of this it would be her. For some reason he saw this as the most productive line of attack. After previous cases she had learnt to trust the man's instincts. He might not be the quickest, the most agile, and was certainly not the most PC detective in the force but his nose was one of the best. He sniffed things before you even had the full picture. The library it would be to keep hunting down Simon O'Neil. Macleod and the team could take care of another body.

Chapter 18

Lilly McGregor was not your typical twenty-year-old. She had no time for clubs, no time for fashion, no time for any of that trivia. From the time she was knee height all she had wanted was to work on the water. A plain girl with short brown hair, she cut an indistinct image, sinewy enough that with her wet gear on it was hard to tell if she was a young man or a young woman. That did not matter to her for she preferred the company of either sex as long as they liked the water. Having completed various journeys on board cruise ships as crew, she was taking some time back home to look after an ill mother and had acquired a job close to the marina in Inverness where there was a station that cleaned the underside of vessels.

It was not as glamourous as the cruise ships she had been on, but then Lilly was not about the glamour. On the ships she had worked on the non-passenger side, hidden away from the paying public but functioning as one of the many crewmates necessary to the safe running of the vessel. Back on dry land she was grateful to simply have a job that was connected with the sea, even if she was not actually out on it.

There was a small cruiser being hauled up the slipway ready for its cleaning of the hull, a necessary task for any vessel but this one seemed to be somewhat more of a mess underneath than one would expect. There was also a rope around the midpoint of the vessel just behind the main structure that ran round three cords thick. Lilly had no idea why anyone would have it there and the master of the vessel, a rather old and somewhat simple man said that was how it had been given to him.

The same master was now standing beside the slipway watching the vessel come out of the water. Apparently, he had been offered a generous sum to simply take the vessel from a mooring just outside Inverness and bring it to the slipway. The current owner, who had failed to mention their name, was unavoidably called out of town and did not want the vessel to miss its appointment. Lilly watched the master as the vessel made its slow progress and saw his eyes start to widen.

The man began to jump up and down and start to wave his hands at the operator of the winch taking the boat from the water. Lilly looked over but Alan was not seeing the man and Lilly waved at him. Alan looked annoyed and stuck his head out of the operator's cabin.

'What the hell's the matter, girl?'

'The master, the old guy's waving like a mad thing.'

'He's probably worried that something's had a slight scrape. Well stuff him, we need to get this boat or we'll never get clear before dark. Bugger him!'

Lilly shrugged her shoulders. She had tried and who cared if she had failed as the key thing was to get done and get home. Looking back at the vessel, Lilly gasped at the state of the hull, the number of barnacles stuck to it along with other debris. And then she saw an arm.

It was not commonplace to find limbs and other body parts

attached to vessels, but it was not unheard of. People were lost at sea and if they did turn up it was usually in the shallow water or on the rocks at the coast. The possibility of them catching onto a vessel was remote, but it did happen.

Lilly was not a woman to panic and simply walked further down the slipway to try and catch a better view of the limb. As she walked down and the vessel moved up, she saw that there was a torso attached to the arm. Next came one of the most horrific sights of her young life. There was a bearded man hanging there, attached by three ropes around him, the very same she had seen wrapped around the boat. And she thought he moved.

Without hesitation she took a knife from her belt and began to cut at the ropes as the vessel moved further on its journey. She could see the man's skin was white and his body inflated slightly but if there was a slight chance he was alive then she would get him down from his torturous position.

Her knife was sharp, but the cord was thick, and it took her a good minute to cut the man off. As the last rope gave way, she tried to catch him, but he fell on top of her and she hit her head on the slipway and found a face with dead eyes looking right at her. Resisting the urge to scream, she pushed the man off her, scrabbling out from under him.

As Lilly looked at the figure now lying on the floor, she saw his back ripped asunder, and wondered if there was any flesh remaining on it. The vessel had stopped its motion and Alan could be heard approaching.

'Oh, my God, shit, Lilly.' Lilly could hear Alan vomiting. But she stood there transfixed by the man's back. Looking up at the hull she saw the barnacles and remembered the tales of the sea she heard as a youngster. Keelhauled, they called it. Pulled round the underside of a vessel, your back ripping open on the barnacles and other shell or debris that was there as you struggled for breath. Done time and again as the salt water stung your wounds and the water carried the blood away all the faster.

Lilly broke her morbid fascination as Alan, spitting out little globules of sick, shouted at her. 'Lilly, 999, get the police! Dear God, get someone!'

* * *

Macleod watched Ross change into a white overall and together they walked over to Jona Nakamura who was studying the body on the ground. Screens had been set up around the vessel on the slipway and when Macleod saw the body of the deceased, he knew why. The back was almost non-existent, torn away. Looking at the hull, he saw skin attached to barnacles which were broken and jagged.

'Inspector, particularly brutal, this one,' said Jona and knelt down beside the body. 'If you look you can see the flesh has been torn away. Keelhauled as they say. Strapped to the underside of the vessel and pulled across it. You would be struggling for air at the same time as your back was ripped apart. The salt water would also get into those wounds causing more pain.'

'"This is how to deal with pirates." That's what it said, Ross. But why is this man a pirate?' Macleod knelt down beside the head and Jona turned it so Macleod could see the face. It was bloating slightly and turning white. But it was no one Macleod recalled.

'Maybe a thief, sir,' pondered Ross. 'Taking something of

someone else's maybe. Pirate is a pretty archaic term so it could refer to a number of things today. Selling dodgy DVDs.'

'You don't get your back ripped off you for selling dodgy DVDs, Ross. Remember, every other victim was a killer. Maybe a violent theft, a killing where something was stolen. I'm struggling to recall a pertinent one and certainly one where I would have forgotten the face. I'm not that senile yet, Ross; I still remember my cases.'

'This one has been dead a while, Inspector,' said Jona. 'Maybe a week because the water's having an effect but certainly not months.'

'Serious planning then, Miss Nakamura. He knew this was coming, ramping everything up. He had to make sure that card arrived, and he knew the original was burnt in the fire. But he had to fake the delivery, throw it in the mail, franked and everything. It's someone in the station, Ross.'

'We have a large number of people working this case who would know about the card being burnt, sir,' said Ross. 'I'll start going through them, see if we have anyone new, anyone from Glasgow, previous with your cases.'

'Quietly, Ross, do it very quietly lest they know we are onto them.'

'Don't forget forensics,' said Jona. 'We have such access and we would have known about the card.'

'Anyone in particular, Miss Nakamura?' asked Macleod.

'No, not a person, Inspector. But thinking about the deaths so far, this is a technical person.'

'Why?'

'When they killed Kyle McAvoy, hung, drawn, and quartered him, you need certain skills to do that, a methodical mind. Lot of blood to clear up, lot of thought about sending packages with body parts so they arrive intact and don't get intercepted. Would you know how to do that?'

'No,' replied Macleod, 'I tend to ask the questions not solve them. Technical matters are your domain.'

'Exactly,' said Jona. 'Take the rats. How long does it take to eat through a person, how long until they die? How long can you keep them from being missing? It's a scary thought but this is second nature to me to think about these things. I know how to assess and judge. With the right access, I can work out most anything.'

'And the pole,' commented Ross, 'that was a technical problem. It has to be strong enough and yet you transport it in a car or small van. You need to be sure, know how it works.'

'And this,' said Jona. 'You need to understand where I will look. Need to know where is safe to leave a card.'

'I had forgotten the card,' mused Ross.

'I hadn't,' spat Macleod. 'It's on the body. That's why the body is so well secured. Look Ross, the back's nearly gone but it was protected, held against the vessel so nothing would come out of the rear.'

'And if you understand that the body is not going to decompose that quickly,' said Jona, 'you can be fairly sure how the discovery of the body will play out. They got it wrong with the electrocution, but then that is more of a specialism. The card got burnt but here it's secured.'

'Where?' asked Ross.

'Inside the body,' said Macleod and gave Jona a nod. Gently she reached into the open back of the man and probed around past the remaining organs.

'Packed up by the heart, Inspector. Give me a minute and

I'll get it out cleanly without damaging the corpse. We'll also need to open it in a clean space so if you go and wait in the evidence tent, I'll join you shortly.'

Macleod nodded and retired beyond the screens and looked for the evidence tent. He had no desire to watch a body being probed and adjusted to release the evidence and the fresh air of the sea was a welcome tonic. Looking beside him, he saw Ross, good old dependable Ross, looking somewhat white.

'You okay, Ross?'

'Yes, just a bit beyond the usual, sir. Does it not get to you?'

'The real horror is yet to come, Ross. I'm dreading what the card will say. But yes, it does affect me. I'm human like you. But if I fall apart, then who do you lean on?'

Macleod said little while they walked to the evidence tent and awaited Jona with the card from the body. When she came, she presented a bloody plastic envelope inside an evidence bag. On a clean table she opened the bag and let the card drop onto the surface. Taking a pair of tweezers, she delicately opened the envelope, careful not to rip the envelope apart. Again, she gently pulled out the card and let it lie on the table. The card had Macleod's name on it and nothing else.

'Flip it over, Miss Nakamura.' Jona did as asked and Macleod found the writing on this new side hard to read. The text was small, unlike previous cards and was probably due to the fact the killer seemed to have a lot to say.

'Read it, Jona, please.'

The Asian woman coughed and then held the card up close to her. 'Macleod, I find you guilty of not delivering a just punishment on those who have caused such misery to so many. Their crimes are well known but yours is not, for you shielded them in the phoney capacity of a public servant. But now

159

everyone will know of your crime because it will be held high like your blasphemy. You'll explain your sin as your woman pays your price for it on your faith's doorstep.'

A chill went through Macleod and he began to stumble. Ross reached forward and steadied him until Macleod pushed him away with a hand. The Inspector reached inside his white coverall and found his mobile, pressing the image of Jane that was displayed.

'Pick up, pick up.'

'We have protection up there, sir. They would have called in,' Ross said, trying to calm his boss.

'Jane, are you okay, love? Yes, I am panicked. Has there been anything unusual? And the officers are outside in the car. Yes, the ones for my security. No, it's fine, love. Take it easy. No, no, it's just the case; I'm fine.'

Macleod closed the call on the mobile. 'Ross, get a car up there and double check. How is he going to do this? Get everyone up there. Lord, help me!'

Ross shouted for a constable and then helped his boss to a seat before departing the evidence tent. Macleod held his head in his hands and stared at the floor. 'How's he going to do this, Jona, how?'

'It's not Jane, sir; it's not your partner,' said Jona holding the card up before her. 'It's not Jane. It says your woman. We don't call Jane your woman; she's your partner—Mrs Macleod if someone is teasing, Inspector.'

'What are you on about, Jona? I've never heard any of this.'

'Of course, you haven't, it's station banter,' said Jona, taking out her mobile. 'She lives with you. Before that she was always around you. You helped her in her difficulty, so everyone saw her as your woman in work. Not your partner but 'your

160

woman', your bit on the side. Of course, it was in jest, but it stuck, the nickname stuck.'

'Who are you on about, Jona?' But then Macleod's face displayed a realisation. Of course, she had been close, been around him and been familiar. He had even used her first name at times. They were similar ages, and people would talk. He looked desperately at Jona.

'It's no good, Inspector, it's going to voicemail. I can't get hold of Hazel. I can't reach Mackintosh.'

Chapter 19

Macleod called his house again and when Jane picked up the call there was no mistaking the anxiety in his voice.

'Where's Hazel, Jane?'

'She went into town, Seoras. Said she had a few things to pick up, but she should be back anytime. She's in her own car. Why? What's up?'

'What time exactly did she say she'd be back?'

'About fivish. Why? What's the matter, Seoras?'

'Hopefully nothing, but don't do anything. Stay inside and keep the doors closed—and locked! There'll be a few more police cars up our way but just stay inside. And don't worry.'

Jane was indignant. 'Don't worry! What does that mean? Of course, I'm going to worry. What's up? Is Hazel all right?'

'I hope so, Jane, but I really have to go. Stay inside and stay safe. Shout the police officers out front if you see anything suspicious.'

'Okay, love. Take care though. I need you back in one piece. Go find Hazel.'

Macleod closed the call and looked across at Jona Nakamura. The forensic lead had kept trying Mackintosh's mobile, but it had kept returning to voicemail. Macleod wondered what to do. If her mobile was going to voicemail then it might have been taken off her. But they could still try pinging it, see if it gave a location. The telephone company could also tell if it was switched off in a normal fashion.

'Ross, get on to the SPOC (Specific Point of Contact) and get Mackintosh's mobile pinged. See where it went off, or if it's still on. Then we need to get to those places to find out if anyone saw her. Also, her car, get a call out for her licence plate and registration. Jona, do you know it?'

'Red Corsa, recent purchase. They'll have her registration at the station for her parking.'

Ross nodded at Macleod and disappeared to his duty. Macleod felt his heart pump fast. Everyone else this man had taken had been killed and brutally. He had dished out maximum pain and now he was determined to visit it on an innocent. Macleod could see that he could be a target but to victimise someone else and someone who was a colleague. Mackintosh never protected people, more often than not she provided evidence that convicted them. And she was a colleague, not his partner. Why had he not gone for Jane?

Macleod's mobile rang and he answered immediately. 'Macleod!'

'Seoras, I just got a text from Ross. Mackintosh is missing. Where shall I meet you?' asked Hope.

'Don't! Stay the course. You need to come after the man from a different angle in case we don't get there, in case we can't find him. I've got this. I'll get Mackintosh, but you keep going.'

There was a silence and Macleod knew Hope would be raging at his decision. Hazel Mackintosh was a colleague, one who had been through the mill with her own medical problems of late and now she was in real danger of losing her life in a violent way. And then came a simple statement. 'Okay, Seoras, you get to it.'

'Inspector, I know the lines you are following but there is another way to look at this,' said Jona.

'How do you mean?'

'The card. He was taunting you on the card. Looking to run you ragged. Give you a little hope. *Listen—But now everyone will know of your crime because it will be held high like your blasphemy. You'll explain your sin as your woman pays your price for it on your faith's doorstep.—"held high like your blasphemy"*; I don't know what that means.'

Macleod shook his head. 'None of it makes sense, Jona. It's a madman.'

'Maybe, but he also has a plan, one that he wants you to follow, so maybe you can. Maybe you can beat him at this. Let me see.' Jona stared at the card and then grabbed a pen writing down words on a pad of paper.'

'What are you doing?' asked Macleod.

'Brainstorming, shush!' The pen flew across the page and every now and then Jona would look up at the inside of the evidence tent. And then she smacked the tip of the pen on the page. *Pay your price on your faith's doorstep*—churches, Inspector, she'll be in a church of some sort. But it'll be some sort of torture. Oh God, no!'

'What?!' cried Macleod. 'What is it?'

'He's going to crucify her! Held high, like Jesus, held high on the cross, like the serpent in the wilderness.'

Macleod needed no references and as soon as she said it, the idea was obvious to him. Time was now against him. If he nailed her to a cross, Hazel would struggle to survive and would endure one of the most torturous deaths known. Crucifixion in the Roman age was barbaric, meant to be so to make a point. Macleod tore out of the evidence tent.

'Stewart,' shouted Macleod across the boat yard, 'get a map of the area!' Walking to his car that was parked close to the slipway, he waited for Stewart to join him and took an OS map from her. 'Churches, Stewart, we need to identify every church in the area and get inside it. I believe Mackintosh is in one of them and time is running out for her. You get every church marked, disused ones as well; we need to cover all bases. I'll get hold of the Chief Inspector. We're going to need as many uniforms as she can give me on this.'

'Every church, sir?' queried Stewart.

'Every single one, Stewart. And quickly. I need to be sending people out fast.' Macleod felt his neck becoming tense and the weight of his task made him shake inside. Shoving his fears to one side, he took his mobile and readied himself for the call he was about to make. He would need to get the entire force moving. But how far out did they go? How far north or south, east or west? Hazel could be anywhere. Jona was probably right on the church idea but this man had killed on the northern coast, halfway down the A9 to the south as well. Start from the centre, Seoras, he told himself. Start here and simply work out. But surely it would be somewhere quiet, after all, the main churches would have people about them.

'Ruins, sir? Do you want me to include ruins as well?'

'Anything you think could be recognised as a church, Stewart.'

Macleod pressed the screen on his mobile and then waited for his boss to answer. The Chief Inspector was a good woman and a fine officer. She came from a time that Macleod understood but she was more adapted to the modern way. In fact, because of the changes that freed women in the workplace, moves that had come over decades, she was now in a role she could have struggled to see all those years ago.

'Macleod. What do you need? You never ring me like this unless it's important.'

'I have one of our own missing and I believe about to be crucified, literally, if she has not been already. I need everyone we can spare, and I mean everyone. I will put the request in for officers, but I need your word from above to get the maximum response.'

'Who's in danger?' asked the Chief Inspector.

'Hazel Mackintosh, Chief Inspector, forensic lead.'

'I know Hazel, Seoras. You said crucified?'

'Yes, I did.'

'I worked with Hazel back in the day, Seoras. One of us. Started at the bottom like ourselves, back when times were different. A tough old bird they would have said back then. Or rather a tough young lass. I'll put the word down, whatever you need; just get her, Seoras.'

'Of course.' Macleod closed the call, his hands shaking. It was on him. The game was afoot. And his woman was depending on him. For a moment he thought about that statement, about Hazel and how they had become closer during her cancer treatment and now as she had been looking after Jane. If Jane had not been in his life, Hazel would have been someone who might have taken that place, who could tell.

Macleod heard Stewart calling over a uniformed officer and patching a link up to the station. She was soon delivering the orders on which churches to send units to. He heard churches from the Inverness area being called out and many of them he knew. Things were in motion and he trusted Stewart to run this and collate everything. Ross would be making sure that Mackintosh's mobile had been pinged and that any sightings or CCTV was being utilised. He'd also have the call out for Hazel's car.

Taking his mobile out again, Macleod called Hope. He'd need to keep her in the loop, but he was also determined that she should not suddenly come back with the news of Mackintosh's abduction.

'McGrath, here.'

'Hope, how far are you off finding our man?' asked Macleod.

'Still tracing him but I'm off to see his work colleagues. I've had some detail on his past, how he's had some sort of abuse, but no one so far has had a picture. I'm off to the library where he used to work to try and get further details or an address. I'm close but not there yet.'

'Stay on it and as fast as you can. Mackintosh has been abducted by our killer. He's going to crucify her, Hope, somewhere in the area in a church.'

'Do you want me to come back?'

'No!' Macleod was insistent. 'Think about it, Hope. He's gone for Mackintosh because he thinks she's my woman. He wrote it on the card he left at another body. One we have found today at the boat yard.'

'Your woman? But that's a joke in the station. Jane's your woman.'

'Exactly. So, it's someone at the station who doesn't know me very well. He's able to see everything we are doing because he's on the inside. He doesn't know about you, so keep going. You can head him off. Everything I'm finding out, is coming through the normal channels and he can see it or get wind of it. But not you.'

'Sounds like he's also dragging you about on the end of a chain. I'd stop that; don't give him the pleasure. He must be watching you squirm at the moment.'

'And do what,' shouted Macleod; 'just sit here and let Hazel die so as not to give him any pleasure?' His voice dropped again to a soft tone. 'Hope, trust me, we have to play along; otherwise, he'll know we have something else. Move fast and tell me if you find out anything. But be quick.'

Macleod paced about watching what was happening and then took a report from Ross about a half hour later. Mackintosh's mobile was still active. It was in the main shopping area of Inverness and close to several churches. Calling for a car, Macleod told Stewart to stay and keep going with her search of all the churches while he would check out this latest development with Ross.

In the car, Ross seemed tense but excited as he drove. Macleod in contrast simply stared out of the window, tapping his fingers.

'She'll be okay, sir,' said Ross. 'We have her mobile contact so we can trace her now. Even if the mobile's not in church, it'll be close by her. Should we go in quietly though, not let him know we are coming?'

Macleod chewed the question over in his mind and then shook his head. 'Make it a full circus, Ross. Everything, lights, sirens, plenty of disruption to the average person. This is his show—do you get that? He's about to make a mockery of us. And as long as he has anonymity then he can do that. He believes we have no idea who he is, doesn't know we know he's among us. If we do anything but play along like we are taken by him, then he'll bolt and we won't get him. But he'll be just as dangerous on the outside.'

'That's a dangerous line to follow. He is a killer.'

Macleod drummed the window beside him. 'Thank you, Ross, I was aware of that. Keep the foot down but I doubt she'll be here. But it does mean one thing if we find the mobile.'

'That he's in the area.'

'Exactly, Ross. And if we can identify him, then we can grab him while he doesn't know we are onto him.'

The centre of Inverness was busy on a shopping day, the tall stone buildings adorned with bright signs and picking up a dreary day for most shoppers. The earlier arrivals of police officers had now cleared a way to the centre of town for Macleod and his cavalcade of cars who were bringing officers to search the area. Looking around, there were two churches in the immediate area, one was the main national church in the town and a large building right on the main street. The other was a small church, almost a sect to some and the building looked more like an office than a church.

'Ross, send the officers into the main church, there's plenty to search for in there. Once they have started, go and see the small Christian charismatic behind us down the alley. It'll be in there. But don't let on you have found it. I'll ring Stewart and tell her to focus the search more locally once you have confirmed the mobile is there.'

Macleod watched the teams enter the main church, let in by an officer of the church. A representative of all churches had been asked to go to their respective buildings and Macleod watched Ross quietly gain access to the other smaller building in the alleyway. Ten minutes later, Ross returned and simply nodded to Macleod.

'Tell me you left it there,' he asked his junior officer.

'It was left out in the open, easy to see, sir. I've hidden it more discreetly, so it'll take a while longer to find.

Macleod called Stewart on his mobile and asked her to start prioritising churches in the Inverness area. But to do it subtly and not pass any word about her reasons to anyone. With that message complete, Macleod stood on the street, eyes on the general public watching the circus. He was in the middle of it and was aware of the eyes on him. This was his punishment, his reward for doing his job and keeping the peace, even in the arrest of those who had done so much harm. Inside, a rage burned but he held his exterior. It was a gamble, and he knew Hazel's life depended on it. Surely the man would make him suffer as much as possible in the public eye. If he could keep that going for as long as possible, then Hope might be able to identify him.

Macleod was not a man to trust many, preferring to hold it all himself but the last year or two had taught him to rely on the small team he had built around him. And today was the time to hold his cards and not play them too early. He'd need Stewart and Ross to get to Mackintosh and then keep it quiet, let the killer think they were still looking. And he'd need Hope to come through. Macleod clinched his fist as he tried to control his nerves. *That's it, everyone, watch me, watch the desperate Inspector. Come on Hope, come through for me! Dear God, let her come through.*

Chapter 20

Hope entered the main library in Inverness and looked for the librarian on duty. The building was located beside the bus station and Hope had walked from a nearby supermarket car park due to the difficulty of parking. She had seen the many tourists and locals scrabbling for the buses and wondered how many of them had this latest set of murders on their lips. The press had gone to town and every paper that she saw had some clever take on the situation.

The murders had been horrific but the degree to which certain papers dwelt on the gore and not the police chase was discomforting. Macleod ignored the papers and had told Hope to do so on many occasions in the past but even he was feeling the pressure they generated.

Walking past the rows of books, Hope found a genteel older lady behind the reception desk. She regarded Hope in her jeans and t-shirt with a little haughtiness but then she must see all sorts coming into the library. There would be those with no discernible job who simply floated throughout the day into places like this which were free to use and were warm. Others would race in during their office break and travellers may even kill time in here during the changeover in their bus journey.

But Hope was not for messing about today. 'DS McGrath, Ma'am.' Hope flashed her warrant card at the woman. 'I'm here on urgent business and need to talk with the manager or the senior librarian about a previous colleague.'

The woman nodded curtly and disappeared through a door into the rear of the building. In a few moments she returned with a younger woman, maybe in her late forties who seemed concerned. 'Hello, Detective, I'm Angela Marshall, head librarian and I believe you require some assistance. If you'll accompany me to my office, I'll see what I can do for you.'

Hope followed the woman up a small staircase and into a tidy office that was decidedly smaller than Macleod's one at the station. Hope was offered a chair and a coffee, the second of which she declined, stating that she was in a hurry.

'Well, Detective, how can I help you?' said Angela taking her seat behind the smart desk at the centre of her office.

'I believe you had a Simon O'Neil working here for a while?'

The woman reared slightly and then composed herself. 'That's right; Mr O'Neil was part of the team here for a while.'

'Would you have a photograph of him?'

'I don't see why we wouldn't, but it would be from his ID badge. It's the only photo we take of the staff unless there's a publicity shot or something of that ilk for a book awareness campaign. But as I recall, Simon was decidedly against posing for photographs.'

Hope sat forward; her interest grabbed at this development. 'Why was that? Little unusual, is it not?'

'Simon was unusual, Detective. Don't get me wrong; as a librarian, he was first class, conscientious with the books and cataloguing, perfectly fine with our customers, although not jovial. But that's not an issue. Margaret downstairs, the

172

woman who got me for you is somewhat stuck up. Actually, she's a snooty-nosed snob in truth but she treats customers well and is good at her job. I don't have an issue with my people if they can cover off the job and look after the customers. What they do in their own time is up to them.'

Hope was now nearly off her seat. 'In their own time? What did Simon do in his own time?'

'He researched medieval times, especially torturers, methods of execution. At least that's what Dawn said.'

'Dawn?' asked Hope.

'Yes, Dawn Gilmartin, she's our youngest librarian. Lovely girl but got some strange habits. Into all that cosplay and stuff. Simon and herself hung out together for a while. I think she fancied him quite a bit, but it seemed to go sour. I'm not sure he was what she was expecting.'

'In what way?'

'Well,' said Angela, almost whispering as if she should not be saying this at all, 'I think Dawn was looking for some bedroom action, or at least some sort of intimacy and I'm not sure Simon was interested. There was a row between them one day downstairs and I had to bring them up here and reprimand them. You can't bring personal lives into work, Detective, certainly not in that way. In fact, thinking about it, Simon was not a typical man.'

'How?'

'Well, you know men, they like to stare at a good-looking woman. But Simon was not interested at all. Dawn, for instance, in the flush of youth, no model but a lovely looking girl, and interested in him. But nothing, not even a glance in that respect. Seemed strange.'

'Some people don't have that side to them though,' said Hope.

'That's true. I wasn't criticising, just making an observation. And I'd say it wasn't that he was interested in his own sex either. Just didn't seem to look at anyone or dream about any person. We're not all googly eyed at someone we dream about but most of us look at sometime or other, will at least have a joke about the latest telly heartthrob. Simon could not handle any conversation like that. It was just a bit weird.'

'Did he have any trauma in his past that might be the cause of it?' asked Hope.

'None I was aware of and certainly he declared none in his application form or in his time here.'

'Can you get me that photograph we talked about at the start of our conversation?' asked Hope. She was sure there was something in this man. Researching medieval times and torturers—surely this was the person they wanted.

She sat impatiently as Angela delved into her computer but then seemed to be somewhat confused. The woman then made a phone call before leaving the room for a moment. On her return, Hope saw she was slightly worried.

'I'm afraid I don't have a picture of Simon. It appears he made a request to our HR department on leaving that his personal information including his ID photograph was deleted. They were holding onto it for a few months after he left but it's now been deleted.'

Hope nearly swore but she thought hard for a moment. 'Did he go out on any work evenings? Out for a meal where someone might have snapped his picture?'

'No,' said Angela, abruptly. 'He didn't attend any of those, not that we have that many, but he was never present. If you want a picture, I think your best bet is Dawn, Detective. She might have snapped him.'

'Do you have her number? I'd like to get hold of her as soon as possible.' Hope tried to hold down her frustration at how long it was taking to get a picture of Simon O'Neil, but Angela could feel her impatience. Then the woman seemed to make a leap in her mind.

'He's not involved with these murders,' said the woman in a horrified tone. 'Surely not. I mean he was . . .'

'Was what?' asked Hope.

'A little weird but . . .'

Hope waited but she saw the realisation in the woman's mind that just maybe Simon was a killer. 'I can't comment on a current investigation, Angela, but I do need Dawn's number and quick. I'd also ask that you do not share our conversation with anyone.'

'Of course,' said the woman but the shock that a former employee may be a killer was still sinking into her mind. She pulled her mobile from her pocket. 'Dawn should be on her way to Cromarty. It's a part-time library and she's covering this afternoon.' Angela held her mobile to her ear but then shook her head. 'She's not answering. Do you want me to leave her a message?'

'Yes, keep trying. Here's my card,' said Hope. 'You can leave my number on the answer machine. Give me the number and I'll try as well. I'm going to head over to Cromarty and catch Dawn there. If you get her, then please ask she contact me immediately.'

Hope thanked the head librarian and then made her way back to her car. The traffic was busy as she headed for the Kessock bridge, making her way across the Moray firth and onto the Black Isle. Cromarty was at the tip of the Isle and it would take a good half hour to get there. The day was now greying, and she wondered if rain was coming.

Hope felt so close to breaking this case. She had her man. Surely Simon O'Neil was the killer; surely his fascination with medieval times made him the prime suspect. But who was he these days? She knew he had come from Glasgow, had changed his name, and was now living up here. Maybe he had realised Macleod was working at Inverness and followed him. If he was taking out *protected* killers as he saw it, then the lengths he would go to would be extreme. And his lack of sexual interest could be from abuse. A number of the murderers the executioner had tortured and killed were abusers of one sort or another.

The Black Isle roads, while reasonable, were all a single carriageway making overtaking difficult on the curving bends. Many were long and sweeping and treacherous if you got your timing wrong during the overtake. And Mackintosh's face kept coming back to Hope. One of their colleagues was in trouble and Hope was Macleod's gambit. She needed this photograph.

Hope remembered Cromarty from staying there during her first mainland case with Macleod. The library was just along from the rented house they had stayed in and the tight streets of Fishertown, the old part of Cromarty where the fisher folk used to live, brought back memories of that first case. They had also worked on finding the killer of a body on the small ferry at Cromarty and so coming back here again seemed to invigorate Hope. They had solved those cases and they would solve this one. But they needed to do it with no more loss of life.

Hope half ran into the small library located beside the town's episcopal church. There were a few locals who looked around at the noisy arrival, but she saw Dawn, or at least who she thought was Dawn Gilmartin, straight away. The young woman was wearing a plain blue t-shirt and a pair of smart black jeans. There was nothing pretentious about her and she looked up at Hope with an encouraging smile.

Hope walked up to the woman and was aware of the faces looking at her. 'Dawn Gilmartin?' The woman nodded. 'DS McGrath, let's find a quiet corner, please.'

Dawn let herself be led by Hope to the far side of the room and stood with anxious eyes. 'It's not Auntie Jane, is it? I told her she needed to be in a home.'

'No, it's not. As far as I am aware, all your relatives are fine. I need some information from you regarding Simon O'Neil. Specifically, I need a photograph.'

'That weirdo. That poor sod doesn't know what he wants.' Dawn's voice was loud, and Hope raised a finger, telling her to keep a hushed tone. The irony of telling this to the librarian was not lost on her.

'Sorry, Detective, I just spent a lot of time on that man and got nothing back. I thought we had something despite his obsessions.'

'Obsessions?' queried Hope.

'Yes, he liked a bit of bondage. Pretend torture. I love some cosplay myself although this was different.'

'Sorry, just slow down a moment,' said Hope. 'I've been a cosplayer and I don't remember any bondage or torture. Back up and tell me from the top. And do you have a photograph?'

'Look, it's quite simple. He was pretty hot in a funny sort of way and I mentioned I liked dressing up one day at work. He was into medieval stuff, always reading about that sort of thing and I have a bit of a thing for dressing up in the old leather garments from the day. So, we started going to medieval events. He was really into the historical aspects but then I noticed it was around the punishments they had. He was big on the mechanisms, how they did it and how it worked on their victims.'

'And you didn't find that a bit strange.'

The girl shook her head and looked around to see if anyone else was overhearing her conversation. 'Don't say this out loud but I kind of liked the whole idea of torture and that. I mean in a fun way, not giving out actual pain, but as a bit of foreplay. I thought I could actually snag him by going along with his interests.'

'But it didn't work out?' said Hope.

'Several times I helped him build some replica machines and then I'd be the maiden on the rack or tied up in ropes. All perfectly safe and that. He'd set it up properly and then make an adjustment, so it was safe. I'd be there wearing not a lot, and pretend to be tortured, losing some clothing as I did it. He was bloody more interested in how the equipment worked than me, looking for some action. Boy, did I pick the wrong one.'

'Do you have any photos of him?'

'I deleted the ones on my phone when I dumped him, or just stopped going to things with him. I'm not sure we were ever an item, not to him anyway.'

'But do you not have anything? I mean did you not record those times when you made the torture devices and that.'

'Sure, but that's not for public consumption, I'm not going to put them on my phone in case it's stolen.'

Wise girl, thought Hope. 'But you did keep them?'

'In my flat, I have a USB stick which has a few of the videos. To be honest, I haven't looked since I realised he was not interested. It's kind of disappointing being there, the forlorn and sexy maiden and he's looking at gears or cogs.'

Hope could only nod. It seemed surreal but it also was right on the money for their killer. 'Lock up, Dawn, we need to go to your flat.'

'But I can't. I need to stay with the library. Mrs Marshall won't be happy.'

Hope gave Dawn a frown. 'I'm running a murder investigation and require your assistance. Everything else can wait.'

The girl looked confused and then something clicked in her head. Hope caught her as she stumbled. Dawn looked up with the question in her eyes. It was one Hope knew the answer to but could not say. But her silence answered it for Dawn and Hope saw the woman begin to panic.

'Don't! Lock up, Dawn. Focus on this. Apologise to your customers and lock up.'

The girl nodded a little too profusely and then Hope watched her announce in broken phrases that the library needed to shut. *She probably thinks she's had a close call,* thought Hope, *but I doubt she was in any danger. Still, makes you think.*

Chapter 21

Hope waited until she had cleared the tight Cromarty streets and reached the shore road, before accelerating the car to a speed well above the limit prescribed by law. There was a need to hurry and her impatience at having to now go somewhere else for a picture of Simon O'Neil was infuriating. Whoever he was pretending to be, he no doubt had different names on different documents, keeping his identity as secret as he could. As she drove, Hope's mind drifted to Mackintosh's plight and she could not help but worry if she were moving quick enough.

Beside her in the passenger seat, Dawn sat shaking. She was obviously thinking back over how she had fancied a man who was probably a killer, how she had put herself in danger without knowing it, and had sought to seduce this monster. Hope felt for the woman because she could not share any information and tell her the truth about how she probably was never in danger. But then again, was that true? If Dawn had stumbled upon a plan or some aspect of the killer's intentions, would she have been the first victim?

'Tell me more about him?' asked Hope to her passenger.

'Such as? You seemed to know him better than I did.'

'Your boss at the library, Angela, said he was a real history buff. What exactly did he look into? What sort of things did he discuss and what did you both go to see? What was on his mind? That sort of thing.'

Dawn shifted uncomfortably and Hope realised the woman was beginning to cry. 'He had this fascination at one point about poles. I remember he was searching out about materials and strengths of poles and metal bars. He had shown me a diagram of how they had propped people up onto them, then let them slide down slowly, killing them as an example. It was at one of those dungeon museums, one of the dark ones. I found it fascinating. But I remember now how he was doing calculations about strengths of materials, asking about what they would have used nowadays if they were to do it.'

The woman stopped talking suddenly and then looked across in horror at Hope. 'The A9, the body on the A9. God, no! It wasn't?' And then she burst into tears. The correct answer from Hope was that she could neither confirm nor deny such a statement as it was part of an ongoing investigation. Instead she stayed quiet because the answer on her face was obvious.

'I know you don't want to think about these things,' said Hope, 'but I need as much as you can remember. Something you say might just save a life. I don't know how exactly, or what I'm looking for from you, but I know that something in there might help, no matter how painful it is to go back over it. So please, Dawn, tell me more? Was it always medieval tortures he was concerned with?'

Dawn shook her head. 'Usually, but not always. I remember he had us pretend to have an electric chair. I was sitting in it and he would talk about where the current would have to go. I know it sounds crazy, but I was there in my underwear and found it kinky. He even teased me with little shocks through wet sponges.'

Hope struggled to focus on the road at this point as it swung along the coast making its way back to towards the A9 and the bridge across the Cromarty Firth. Dawn lived in Culbokie, just prior to the A9 and Hope was giving the car everything to get there while listening in horror to the woman's revelations. But so far everything was tying up.

'What other tortures did he try to copy?' asked Hope.

'He became obsessed with crucifixion at one point. I've always found the whole church and pain thing erotic,' said Dawn, and Hope found it hard not to reel in surprise. Hope wore a cross around her neck at times. Originally as a fashion piece but after working with Macleod for so long it had taken on more meaning, although she did not assign it any real status. But it was never erotic. Macleod would have struggled to not lecture Dawn on the blasphemy of what she had just stated.

'He made a cross and I would hang on it for him,' continued Dawn.

'Hang on it?' said Hope. 'How? I thought they nailed Jesus to the cross.'

'They did but that was not common. Simon would tie me up and watch me. I was never up there for more than an hour at the most. It's very painful hanging. We had a safe word and every time I used it, he would release me. Do you see that's why I'm not understanding this? Simon was like me, interested in this stuff and you might find that weird. But he never hurt me. At least not without my consent. And if it was too much, he stopped.'

Hope enjoyed a lot of things in life. She had dressed up at cosplay events, got reckless on beach holidays, and she enjoyed a bit of play in the bedroom but what she was hearing seemed crazy. If it had not been for the man's real intent in performing these activities, then she would have burst out laughing. Instead, she felt numb and could only wonder how Dawn felt.

'I remember,' said Dawn through tearful eyes, 'he was trying to get me to stay up on the cross for longer, like he was working out what effect it had, how long I could last. There's something wrong with me, isn't there? I mean, I enjoyed that, having him watch me. I thought he was enjoying my body, my . . . God, I was just his toy, his crash test dummy.'

The analogy was too good. Hope wondered how someone could be so blind but then she had been besotted before in her life. Not that she had ever gone to such lengths for someone. There was definitely something dysfunctional going on even if the man Dawn had dated had not been a killer. And when he hadn't given her sex, hadn't something clicked. Hope was desperate to ask her how she had not realised but at this time, the question would not help. Instead she pushed for other tortures they tried.

'The only one where I got really hurt was the oil. He would boil up oil and then put little drops on my skin.'

'Did he ever do anything to himself?' Hope blurted out. 'I mean you simply suffer, and he just watches. Did you never think that maybe something wasn't quite right?' It was not the statement she wanted to make having just concluded that she needed to not pursue such a line of attack. And it simply made Dawn break into a pitiful weeping.

'I was in bloody love with him. I was in my underwear when these things happened. They were erotic, exciting, not barbaric. Can't you see that?'

Hope could not, try as she might. The detective mind in

183

her was flagging up that oil had not been used so far and she was fighting not to see that as a punishment being kept for Macleod. After all, he was the focus of the killer's wrath so far. At least according to the cards.

'Did he ever talk about or look to purchase some cards with you, blank ones, dinner card style that you would write a guest's name on.' Dawn shook her head and then folded her arms up around her chest, burying her face into them.

Hope's mobile rang and hitting the hand's free button she took the call. 'McGrath here, currently transporting a witness.' She said this to indicate she was not on her own and able to discuss things candidly.

'Macleod. Do you have anything yet?'

'I have a lot of story, sir, but no positive ID yet. I'm en route to get a picture of our man but it'll be another ten minutes at least. Anything on the forensic front?' Hope knew Macleod would understand she meant Mackintosh and not a laboratory discovery.

'Everything's in motion but not yet. Stay silent and as soon as you have the ID, ring me.'

Hope indicated she would and closed the call. It took another fifteen minutes to arrive at Dawn's house. The simple bungalow was on an estate on the edge of Culbokie and no one batted an eyelid as the pair of them drove into the short driveway. Hope let the woman fumble for her keys and enter the house. A cat ran across Hope's path as she followed, and she called after Dawn who had headed along the entrance hall.

'Where's the pictures?'

'In the back room, I think, on a data stick. I'm looking for it now.'

Hope continued along the hall and entered a room that

looked like a bomb had exploded inside it. There were papers everywhere and many items from shelves had fallen on the floor.

'Sorry,' said Dawn, on her hands and knees,' the cat's new. Got her after I ditched Simon and she gets a bit crazy sometimes. The stick's here somewhere. I'll find it for you, don't worry.'

'I'll help,' said Hope and dropped to her knees and began to lift up piles of papers and shift them to one side of the room. 'Make sure we have some sort of order to this,' she said, 'otherwise we'll just be throwing the same stuff back on top of what's already there.'

Dawn was crying again, and Hope wondered what had set her off again. 'Sorry, all you need is a photo and I can't even get bloody that for you. After all I've done to help that bastard and I can't even show you his face.'

'Enough,' shouted Hope. 'Stop getting caught up in this self-pity. All I need is to find this stick and see Simon's photo. People are depending on you.' It was unprofessional but Hope was at the end of her tether and she hadn't realised just how much Mackintosh's predicament was affecting her. Hope began to throw items across the room, piling them to one side as Dawn became a blubbering wreck. Hope had no time to sit and be a surrogate mother; instead, she tore into the items on the floor. After ten minutes, she stood up, pushing back the sweat on her face.

Macleod's depending on me, she thought. *Mackintosh is depending on me and all I've got is this stupid girl and her bloody cat that's caused havoc. Come on, Hope, come on, you need to get this together. Search, dammit!*

Just then her mobile vibrated and she looked at it to see a

message from Macleod. *Think we may have her. On my way to Urquhart Castle.*

'Thank God,' said Hope out loud.

'What?' asked Dawn, still snivelling.

'I think we may have rescued someone. But we're not done here, Dawn. Sorry if I've been harsh but please, search. We need to find this stick.'

Dawn started to search again, moving things aside and Hope joined her. Soon, over half the floor was clear and Dawn cried out.

'There! I think that's it. Quick, switch on the computer.'

Hope nearly cursed the woman. Why hadn't she switched it on when they had been searching? But Hope did not have anything else to stick the data stick into. Her phone had no port that large and so she had to wait patiently.

As the computer screen changed colour, Hope paced the room crunching her feet onto the piles of paper scattered about. The cat came in and tried to push itself up against Hope's legs. She wanted to pick it up and throw it out of the window as the bloody animal had delayed them already with its stupid destruction of the room. If she had not thought that giving the animal a boot would have set Dawn off again, then she would have happily laid her footwear into its side.

'Right here we go,' said Dawn, in an almost jolly tone. Maybe it was the fact she was at the end of the ordeal; glad this was coming to an end. Either way, Hope leaned over her shoulder and watched as she clicked through pictures on the screen. She saw Dawn in various devices, scantily clad and seemingly in pain. If this was erotic, she was never going after a man again.

And then she saw a man in the background of a picture. He

was kneeling down, his thin spread of hair was showing, but the face was looking down, and hence out of Hope's sight.

'More,' cried Hope,' show me more.'

The pictures flew by, all containing Dawn in her bizarre enjoyment until there suddenly appeared a photograph of the thin haired man. Hope literally gasped as she saw it. She had spoken to the man not long ago. And it clicked with her, all suddenly making sense. A forensic mind, a former librarian. Someone who could be there, delving into records without anyone batting an eyelid. He was filing, putting reports away, calling up others for his boss. And Hope suddenly thought of Jona at the house when they were having dinner, speaking of her day. Every now and then this man's name was mentioned. He was useful, helping out, fetching this detail and that. He had a mind of a forensic investigator, she had said.

A hand flew to her mouth as she realised Macleod had been right. The man had been on the inside. Looking from the screen at her was the face of Elijah Cunningham, Jona Nakamura's newest recruit.

Chapter 22

Macleod put his mobile back into his pocket and bemoaned the lack of progress Hope had made in his head. He wasn't angry at her, but he had prayed that she would have come up with their killer by now. He knew the man was amongst the policing community but just where had left Macleod at a loss.

Stewart was busy covering off all the churches, sorting out which had been visited. Ross had checked Macleod's house and the officers protecting it before assisting Stewart in organising the search. Every possible sighting or strange report to the Police Scotland was being filtered their way. It was a waiting game that Macleod had played before but never had he had a colleague on the line in this way. Sure, they had been attacked at times; sometimes they had been in danger as they pursued suspects but this was the first time someone he had worked with had been kidnapped and threatened with death, and a horrible death at that.

Hazel Mackintosh had been a stroppy forensic examiner who had been more than a match for Macleod and when she had taken a fancy to him in a more-than-professional way, he had remained clear. But she had always held an attraction. And with her cancer diagnosis and subsequent recovery at his house, Hazel had become a friend to both Macleod and Jane. There was a hollowness in his stomach he had never felt before.

'Sir,' shouted Ross, 'over here.'

Macleod strode over to the van from which Ross and Stewart were now operating. 'What have you got, Ross?' Macleod hoped he did not sound desperate.

'Got a sighting of someone hanging at Urquhart Castle, Drumnadrochit, sir. Seen by a boat on Loch Ness and they think they have heard struggling but they are not sure. Called in to the coastguard who fed it through to us. We're sending cars now.'

'Is there a church there?' asked Macleod.

'No idea,' said Ross and reached over and tapped Stewart who had a headset on. 'Urquhart Castle, Kirsten, is there a church in it?'

'There's a chapel, well, what was a chapel as they reckon. It's just a load of stones now and a small hill.'

Macleod stepped away and thought for a moment. Ross was watching him with a strange look on his face.

'It'll be fine, sir. We'll get cars there pretty quick and if Mackintosh is there, we'll get her down. But it might be nothing. They said they could hear things.'

'Can't we just call the office? I mean, it's a tourist site.'

'I did try, sir, but it's closed for renovations. But there was a delay, so there's no one on site,' said Ross.

'How long ago was this known?'

'Been like that for over a week, sir.'

Macleod took Ross aside and whispered in his ear. 'This is a setup, Ross, I'm sure of it. All along I've been the target and now he's going to come for me. But I'll draw him out. He's

189

used Mackintosh and now he'll finish it. If she's alive, it will be to draw me to her so he can finish it. I'm sure of it. I'll go to her now so he's off guard and having to rush his plans forward. He'd expect me at the site but not as the first response. Make sure everyone knows I'm going. We'll see if we can spot him moving. Look for anyone heading that way who shouldn't.'

'Surely best to see if Mackintosh is fine and then stay put. Best not to put yourself in danger.'

Macleod shook his head and stared at Ross, grimacing. 'If he goes back into the shadows he'll come again at others. He wants me for whatever ill I have done him in the past, so we need to end it before others get hurt. This is what he wants so let's try and throw him off a little by upsetting his timescale. I'm going; so get me a car and keep your eyes peeled.'

Within a minute, a patrol car was waiting for the Inspector and he stepped into the passenger seat, urging the driver to take him to Urquhart Castle and not to spare the horses. There was a smile in his face, a protective mask that covered his terror at what they would find. Hazel had to be okay, had to be!

The day was beginning to darken as clouds railed in and spots of rain began on the car's windscreen. With blue lights flashing and a siren going off whenever they encountered traffic, the vehicle sped its way out of Inverness and alongside Loch Ness. Macleod had made his play and now he had to simply wait as he was transported to the scene of what he prayed would be the rescue of Hazel Mackintosh.

As the car turned into the car park at Urquhart Castle, Macleod saw the heavens open and rain began to pour down. There was little wind but the rain fell heavily. Ahead of him, Macleod could see officers running inside the stone walls that surrounded the castle. A long path led from the car park down to the side of the castle before it turned towards the ruin. Running as if his life depended on it, Macleod made his way, ignoring the rain beating down on his head. He crossed the bridge of stone with the wooden fence at its edges running along the neat concrete that was now becoming soaked. The concrete became wooden planks as he continued along the bridge before large paving slabs were underfoot.

Before him, the stone walls of the castle were interrupted by an archway and he desperately hurried through it, the rain being interrupted for a moment and then coming down on his head again. But as he emerged from the archway, he barely felt the rain as he saw several officers before him trying to uproot a wooden cross. Looking up, he saw the figure of Mackintosh, her eyes closed, and her arms and shoulders dipped down. Her feet were twisted, and her knees looked as if they were locked in a bent position and barely supporting her.

He joined the men before him as they pulled away stakes driven into the ground beside the cross, holding it in position. As they freed these, the cross threatened to tumble, but between them the eight or so officers managed to first lift the cross and then gently lay it down. Mackintosh was barely murmuring, and Macleod forced himself to stand clear as better trained officers cut her bonds and administered first aid. Soon a team of green-clad paramedics rushed past him and began to package her onto a stretcher. He grabbed the stretcher along with other officers and they carried Mackintosh to the ambulance at the carpark.

As he saw the blue lights of the ambulance carry away his friend, Macleod looked around him. *Come on, it's me you want. Where are you? What do you have for me?* But there was just more rain. He watched every officer close to him, suspicious of them all but no one put a step out of line. There in the rain, Macleod wondered if he had got it wrong. Had he spooked the man by being so aggressive to the scene? Or had he simply been wrong and his time in the spotlight was for another day?

* * *

Hope picked up her mobile and placed a call to Macleod. It simply went through to his answerphone. She tried again but got the same result. So, she tried Ross who answered on the first attempt.

'Hi, Boss, the inspector's not here. He went down to a report we got from Urquhart Castle. We think that's where Mackintosh is. He might be tied up with that.'

'It's Elijah Cunningham, Ross. I've tracked him through from that early case. His real name is Simon O'Neil, but he's doing this because he was abused, and the Inspector shielded the abuser during the arrest. He doesn't think justice was done so he's carrying it out now.'

'I'll get on to it,' said Ross. 'We'll go for his home and the office.'

'I spoke to him earlier on today and he was in work. Ring Jona as she should know what he's up to. But keep it quiet lest he runs, Ross. Just a select few or he could disappear and given his track record, he's damn good at disappearing into the everyday world.'

Hope hung up the call and looked at Dawn on the floor beside her. The woman was a mess and Hope felt she should try to help the woman given all she'd been through. There was little else for Hope to do and she could spare an hour before heading back and sorting out the inevitable interviews.

Finding the kitchen in the bungalow, Hope switched the kettle on and hunted around until she found two mugs and a teabag. Once the kettle had clicked, signalling the boiling had finished, she made the tea by dunking the bag into the hot water in each cup and then brought it through to the rear room they had been searching in.

'Here,' said Hope, 'I think you could do with this. Sorry, I was pretty harsh, but we needed to get the information and that picture. You can rest now though as it's over—well, as good as. You'll need to make statements and that, but we'll keep your part in his life discreet. There's no need for you to be paraded for the public. We'll certainly do our best on that front.'

Dawn took her tea but said nothing. Instead the woman looked around her at the mess on the floor. She began to pick up a novel that was under some sheets of paper and turned it over in her hands.

'What's that?'

'Just a story he bought me,' replied Dawn. 'You'd probably find it weird; it's erotica with a lot of bondage.'

'Like *Fifty Shades*?'

'No, not like *Fifty Shades*. This is pretty full on. There's a love quadrangle. Two men and two women and a lot of sex in the pages.' Dawn laughed. 'More sex in here than I had with him. But he was keen on the book. Said it had inspired him. I always thought he meant the bondage aspects. I used to sit and read this in bed, imagining me in a lot of the scenes with him. You must think I'm crazy.'

'I didn't say that. It's not for me but whatever floats your boat. I don't blame you for looking for some love, whatever way you like it. You just got the wrong guy big time.' Hope thought

Dawn had been more foolish than that but at the moment, the woman had a low enough opinion of herself without Hope depressing her more.

'He said it had a brilliant plot, but I never saw that. It's pretty stupid really.'

'How do you mean?' asked Hope sipping her tea.

'Well, you have these two couples, and they start playing games and that, swapping over. Well two of the women start to enjoy the same guy.' Hope struggled not to laugh. 'But then the guy on the outside he gets a bit pissed at this, so he decides to have his revenge. He sends the other guy on a chase to save his lover, the other man's wife. But the thing is, all the time he has the man's real wife and ends up killing her while the guy is off saving the other woman.'

Hope dropped her tea and ran for the door.

'Detective? Detective?' Dawn got up and ran down the hallway after Hope who had fled out of the door. As Dawn followed through the open door, she saw Hope's car spinning round and driving off at speed. Confused, Dawn paddled out onto the driveway as the rain beat down upon her. What had she said?

Chapter 23

Hope put the blue flashing lights on in the car as she sped out of Culbokie. With her other hand, she pressed the hands-free button on the car and called out Macleod's name to the phone. She heard the ringing tone as she approached the traffic calming measures at the edge of the village.

'Macleod. Hope, we've got her. Ross said you—'

'Shut up, Seoras. It's not Mackintosh. It's Jane, his plan is Jane. I'm on my way but call the—shit!' Hope saw the other car coming through the one-way section. It was the other car's right of way but Hope had sirens on and lights flashing. Throwing the wheel to the left, she mounted the pavement and smacked a bin sending it rolling into a fence. Her back wheels slid as she fought to control the car and it bucked as it caught a driveway curb. Hope had no idea if the wheel had been damaged but she was not waiting around to find out. Steering the car back onto the road she put her foot to the floor again.

'Are you okay?' came Macleod's concerned voice.

'Yes, but it's bloody Jane he wants. Get there, Seoras. I'm on my way but alert the officers outside. He's coming for Jane.' With that, Hope hung up and focused on her driving as she reached the A9. Without waiting, she raced into the carriageway and began speeding past the cars in front. She saw them part like a wave and her hands gripped the wheel tight. She could make out the scraping sound of a rim and believed she may have bent it a touch causing it to scrape but there was no time to look. A written-off car at the end would be a small price to pay for Jane's life.

The A9 approached the roundabout at Tore, a large circle which Hope was able to drive out onto at speed. Macleod and Jane lived on the Black Isle close to the Moray Firth and the roads to it were single track once you got off the A9. As Hope tore off the main road, she slowed only slightly, aware that if anyone were coming the other way, she could cause a serious accident.

The rain made the road slippery and Hope fought the car at every corner. She was a competent driver, trained in the skill of advanced driving, but she did not race off in pursuit every day and so her heart was racing and her hands were clammy. Inside her stomach, she felt a hollowness. This was not simply a colleague like Mackintosh; this was Seoras's Jane, and her death would kill him. He had been wrong, gamble the man would come for him, happy in the protection provided for Jane. But was it enough? As Hope approached the house, she hand silenced the siren and she extinguished the blue flashing lights.

Before the house was a police car, sitting impassively. Hope pulled up beside it and saw two officers lying back in their seats. She jumped from the car and opened the door quietly. Checking for a pulse, she found it to be weak, but the man was breathing. His female colleague over from him was in a similar state. Hope noted the coffee lying spilt across their laps.

A second police car was sitting further back and slightly off the road. Hope ran to the car and found two male officers in the same predicament as those in the first car, coffee spilt across their laps. Grabbing her mobile, Hope called Macleod again.

'Macleod. Have you got her?'

'Hurry, Seoras. And bring an ambulance.'

'What about Jane?' shouted the Inspector down the phone.

'Unknown, I'm about to go inside. But there's four incapacitated officers outside breathing poorly. Ambulance and back up.'

'We're not far off, Hope, Maybe five minutes. Don't risk it, the man's a killer. Wait for us.' The voice was cracking. Macleod was being professional, looking out for his colleague, making sure she was safe, following protocol despite the obvious anguish he must be in.'

'Like hell, Seoras. This is Jane we are talking about. I'm going in. Hurry!'

Before Macleod could answer, Hope closed the call. Her heart was thumping but she was determined not to let Macleod down. The rain lashed down but Hope only felt a cold sweat across her brow as she realised she would be charging into the lion's den. If she were quiet, maybe he would not hear her coming. Then again, he may already be watching her.

Hope trusted her skills in hand-to-hand combat. She had trained in self-defence and then in dealing with abusive and violent offenders. Compared to Macleod, she was better equipped to handle this killer, but she still felt cold as she made her way through the rain. Get this wrong and she would be dead. Be too slow and Jane would be dead.

Rather than run down Macleod's driveway and give herself

away by the crunch of her boots on the path, Hope ran across a rough lawn. It was uneven and she fought to keep her balance as she moved from one tree to another, trying to stay hidden on approach to the house. Hope had been at Macleod's on many occasions and she knew the rear door was often kept open. Surely Macleod would have told Jane to keep it all locked. But there was the spare key, out by the shed, in the coded lock box.

Hope ran across the drive and hid behind the shed. She placed her arm around the corner of the wooden structure and with her hand located the lock box. Juking her head round, she adjusted the code quickly and opened the black container to find a rear door key to the house. She moved around the shed, keeping it between herself and the house and then approached over open ground to the rear door.

It was locked. Carefully, Hope slid the key into the lock and opened it. It made a gentle click and she scanned through the glass door to see if there was anyone approaching. When she realised no one was coming, Hope pulled the handle down and stepped inside the kitchen. Almost subconsciously she began wiping her feet on the mat. Jane kept the house neat and she always felt bad coming into someone's abode if she were about to mess up a clean floor. The ground from the car to the kitchen had been mucky and now she automatically made sure she was clean before going further.

Bloody hell, Hope, she thought; *what are you doing? Just settle and find Jane. Nice and quiet. Come on.* The kitchen was large, and Hope wondered where Elijah Cunningham would be. It was then she noticed the car parked at the furthest point of the driveway. She had not clocked it before because no one left the car that far away, it was beyond the kitchen and meant you simply had further to walk back. But that was the point.

Cunningham's car was hidden from the road. No doubt he would be escaping in it and then burning it. After all, you would leave tyre tracks here. Or maybe it was not his car.

Hope stole across the kitchen, listening to the sounds of the house but all she could hear was a radio in a distant room. How would he kill her? What method could he bring to the house? Hope recalled her conversation with Dawn. Oil, he had mentioned oil. Cunningham had not used oil yet, but he would need to bring that with him, after all Macleod would not have buckets of it lying around. Opening the kitchen door, she peered into the hallway beyond. At the end on the left would be the stairs to the upper floor. Up there the house had a bathroom that contained a bath you could almost dive into. Creeping along the hallway, Hope opened the doors along it as she passed. The lounge was clear, and the cupboard under the stairs. A reception room near the front was clear, as was the porch. Was she too late? Had Cunningham run? Or had he achieved his purpose?

Climbing the stairs, she placed her feet on the outside of each step, but the wooden staircase still creaked. Her eyes were fixed on the upper floor and as she got near to the landing, she braced herself for an attack. Surely, he must know she was coming.

As Hope reached the top step and then stood on the landing, something caught her eye. Trailing from the main bedroom was a thick black cable that led out of sight around the corner. Hope braced herself up against the wall and then slid along until she came to the corner. The black cable went round there, and she peered gingerly. She was half expecting something to hit her, but nothing happened, and she drew in a breath and made her way around the bend. The cable was running into the bathroom and Hope reached out with a hand pushing back the door.

From her vantage point, Hope saw the toilet with the seat down. She remembered Macleod commenting to her once how Jane had been particular about this and of course, Macleod as a man was prone to leaving it up. Almost against her will, she grinned at his annoyance at this, but she soon found herself wondering if someone was behind the door.

Hope stepped forward, placing a hand on the door and pushed it hard. If anyone had been behind, they would have been smacked in the face by the door and crushed up against the wall. But the door instead hit a spring, causing it to bounce back. Hope's steady hand caught it and gently opened the door fully.

In front of her she saw the bath and it had a golden tinge to it. Behind the wall as she entered stood a number of large oil cans, ten litre drums of vegetable oil. Looking at them she smelt the air and the whiff of something cooking came to her. Taking a bar of soap off the wash hand basin opposite the bath, Hope dropped it into the oil and heard it begin to fry. A long black cylinder was also in the bath and this was attached to the cable she had seen running from the bedroom. Cunningham was going to cook Jane.

But the bath was empty and so Jane must still be alive. Maybe she was close. There were two other rooms on this floor and Hope would need to search both of them, knowing that the killer was probably in one of them. Stepping out from the bathroom, Hope looked at the two remaining doors. The main bedroom was slightly open as the cable was running from it and Hope chose this first. Again, she opened the door with a shove and this time crouched and ran in. Eyes whipping round, she saw no one. The bed was disturbed, and she saw clothes, presumably belonging to Jane lying in a heap on the floor. Some had been cut from the woman.

Standing upright, Hope returned to the hall and then placed a hand on the door to the spare bedroom. Opening it gently she peered in from outside. There was a foot on the bed. It looked like an older person's and she guessed Cunningham would not be running around in a lack of footwear. As she stepped quickly into the room, she saw the shadow move and threw her arms up above her.

The blow was from some sort of heavy metal object, but her arms took the brunt of the attack. Hope still reeled from the attack, falling off to one side but managed to turn herself so she was on her back as the face of Elijah Cunningham dove down upon her. He was not the largest of men, but he was driving a wrench at her face, one that could be used for adjusting the sort of rims a tractor tyre would use. Again, she threw her arms up and felt the crack on her forearm. Had something broken? She had no time to worry and she fought to ignore the pain in her arm as she kicked out hard at the man's kneecap. This forced him to stumble backwards and Hope half got to her feet as he attacked again. She was not in a good position to defend herself and so drove forward, catching him in the stomach with her shoulder and driving him into the wall. But he brought the wrench down on her head and she fell down, groggy and struggling to understand quite how she was orientated.

A hand grabbed her by the hair and she caught a brief glimpse of Jane, lying on her bed, stripped and tied up. The woman was white as a sheet and Hope could see tears in her eyes. Her own were bleary and Hope screamed as her ear was caught in something metal. Maybe he had attached the wrench to her.

Dragging Hope to her feet, Cunningham pulled her out of the room. Hope could feel her ear rip and she screamed out in pain. But she fought hard, pulling away from the man. Her ear was ripping but that would be a small price to pay for her life. And then the ear was released. Hope felt the pain subside until she was struck on the back of the head with the wrench. She fell to the ground and Cunningham pummelled the wrench into her back. Hope heard Jane try to shout but she must have been gagged because the yells were muffled.

Again, her ear was placed in the wrench and she was hauled to her feet. This time she struggled to fight and found herself half stumbling, half pushed out into the hall. From there, Cunningham pushed her into the bathroom before driving her to the ground. Her ear was released and she was dragged by her hair to a standing position. Hope swooned and she felt like she was about to be sick. The air was filled with the smell of vegetable oil and Hope almost thought she was in a chip shop.

As she began to focus, she saw Elijah Cunningham standing before her. Stumbling backwards, she felt the edge of the bath and realised he was going to shove her into it.

'I've never seen anyone fry, never seen how they scream. You deserve it though. Just like him when I saw you. Thick as thieves, and he likes you. Always an eye for you. Trust you with everything. You'll become like him, protecting the killers while the abused suffer. Well, now he can suffer. I'll fry his favourite partner and then fry his woman. And he can come in here and watch. I guess you've called him. No time to lose then.'

Cunningham stepped forward hands out. With a determined effort, he tried to push hard at Hope. Something inside her reacted and she bent down, almost in a fall and he tipped over her. And then she instinctively drove upwards, fearing he would simply collapse on top of her. He slid off of her back and she heard him hit the oil in the bath. The man screamed and she turned around, watching him writhing in agony.

Something inside said she had to get him out. Despite the fact he was trying to kill her, she needed to help him. The skin seemed to crack under the oil and bubbles, small but rapid and many in number, poured around the edge where the skin broke the surface of the oil.

Hope grabbed a towel from behind her and wrapping her arms in it, she tried to grab his arms as they flailed above the oil. She got one and began to haul him, but he slipped back. He was still flailing, and oil flopped out of the bath onto the carpet below. As the other hand thrashed out of the oil, Hope managed to grab it and she pulled him as hard as she could. His shoulder cleared the top of the bath and she wrapped the towel in her other hand and quickly grabbed the legs, tugging tight. She stumbled back, letting him go and the man fell off the bath onto the floor while she tumbled across the room hitting the wash basin on the other side. Quickly she grabbed more towels and leant down over him, trying to wipe the oil off his bare skin. But a hand shot up, grabbing her cheek. The hot oil seared her face and she thrashed at him, tearing herself away. She heard cries of 'Burn, burn' as she tumbled out of the bathroom door and collided with the wall on the far side. And then there were footsteps.

'Hope, are you all right? Where's Jane?'

Hope managed to point in the vague direction of the bedroom, but she then tried to wipe her face; it was burning. Someone turned her over and began to work on her face but all she felt was pain. And then a needle. Somehow the pain subsided slowly, and she closed her eyes.

'The man's frying,' she heard Macleod say and then he was beside her. 'Look after her, get her to hospital, now.' Her eyes opened and she saw a concerned face.

'I got her, Seoras,' she said. But it was barely a whisper and Hope was unsure if he had heard her before her eyes closed again.

Chapter 24

Macleod watched Jona Nakamura as she sat on the heather and stared out over the firth below. There was a crisp wind, not strong but certainly cold. Jona was wearing a large coat that resembled a duvet and had a single wrap-around band which ran across her forehead and over her ears. She did not look cold, in fact was almost serene. Macleod was freezing. Despite being wrapped up in so many layers that he struggled to move freely, the cold air was numbing his feet and legs.

The away day had been Ross's idea. The man had observed that the team were struggling with the end of this last case and needed to engage the issue. The idea of a sharing day had not appealed to Macleod who had insulated himself from any thought about what had happened. Instead he had thrown himself into caring for Jane, and to another degree, Hazel Mackintosh.

Jane was struggling with being in the house. Hazel had remained with her when Macleod went back to work but there had been occasions of screaming and floods of tears in the rear bedroom, and when in the bathroom. Their happy home, picked out by Jane, had been violated and Macleod wondered if they would have to move.

The other issue was that Jane was wary when Macleod went to work. She had always been proud of him but now she worried overtly. In the past he never saw her concern although it was surely there. Now he could see the terror in her eyes when he went to work. If he was a minute late, she was ringing. If he forgot to check in at lunch or dinner time, she was on the phone. A woman who had helped him to relax was now almost paranoid. Not that he could blame her.

Hazel Mackintosh was the surprise. The woman had just survived cancer and now had suffered crucifixion. But she was proving to be stronger than Macleod had ever imagined. Sure, she was seeing a lot more of Jona, leaning on her former charge and friend. But she was also back to that woman he had first come across. Dominant in company without being a pain, and now tender when one to one. She had helped him enormously with Jane, and he could not help but find a space for Hazel in his heart.

Ross called over to his boss, advising Macleod that the bacon was ready. Along with Stewart, Ross had carried a gas cooker up to the top of Fyrish, a local viewpoint and historical site, and was now sitting at a small camping table, making rolls filled with salad and the alluring bacon. At least someone on the team was feeling normal.

Beside Ross, Stewart was pouring coffee. Thankfully, she had not been at the rough end of this case, for she had her own demons to battle from previous episodes. She was on the mend and had bounded up the hill with a rucksack on her back Macleod struggled to pick up. He was getting old, being outgunned by the juniors.

His eyes scanned across to the woman standing at the large stones that dominated Fyrish and his heart sank. Hope was wrapped up like a nuclear winter was approaching and Macleod frowned at this. Not that she could not choose what to wear but this was not Hope. Before she had always cut a look, but now she appeared to be hiding.

Taking two rolls from Ross and then balancing two coffees, Macleod stumbled his way over to where Hope was standing. Sitting down, he handed her the roll and coffee which she took before looking away from him, out into the distance. Her hair was out of its ponytail and blowing across her face. She made no move to clear it from her eyes.

'I'm sorry.'

'Sorry? Why?'

'I got it wrong, Hope. I was sure he was coming for me, so obsessed with him. I never really listened to you. You saw the threat to Jane.'

'But you had the cars up there. I got lucky, finding out his plan. It was a lucky find in a casual conversation.'

'Stop! It was your nose, the detective in you. Always pushing on, even when it looks like it's over.'

Hope turned for a moment, her red hair dragged across her face. 'Well, I guess I learned that from you. You trusted me. I couldn't let you down. I'm only glad I got to Jane.'

'And you are angry,' said Macleod softly.

'Not that that's any use. I killed him. He died in the boiling oil. Probably deserved it.'

'But you're still angry. You think he's made you a killer. And you think he's ruined you. Your carefreeness, your beauty.'

Hope turned away. She ate a piece of bacon roll, followed by a splash of coffee. 'Go and join the others,' said Hope. 'They need their boss after this one. I'll be over.'

'Why are you wearing that coat? With a body like that, why

are you wearing that duvet of a coat? Can't see your curves, your shapes.'

'Sir!' said Hope loudly, then turned away again.

Macleod reached up and turned Hope's chin towards him. With his other hand, he swept her hair back revealing a deep scar running up one side of her face. The skin was twisted, pocked in places. 'He didn't kill you, McGrath; why are you letting him?'

Hope grabbed Macleod's hand and turned away. 'Who's going to want a face like this? Who's going to care about the woman when you have to look at this? You get your woman back and I end up alone, a freak now.'

The rest of the team suddenly went quiet and Hazel Mackintosh came running over. But Macleod stuck out a hand behind Hope, waving Mackintosh away.

'I would. Any sensible man would. You're more beautiful today than when I first met you.' And then in a quiet whisper only Hope and he could hear, 'And you know you turned my head then.'

'And?'

'And so, don't let him win. Don't deprive the world of that carefree woman who challenges what I believe, who is a standard for the likes of Stewart. The person who is a colleague like none other to this team. Don't let Jona lose her friend. Be Hope and let us lift you when you drop. We're a team. Why do you think Ross has us up here? It wasn't my idea. Can you imagine me suggesting a team day out?'

He saw the hint of a smile on Hope's face. It was the first in a while. Again, he reached up and turned her face to him. 'I mean it, don't let him kill you. The world could do with a beautiful woman.' Pushing back her hair he saw the tears flooding into her eyes and her shoulders slumped. With loud sobs, she began to cry, and he held her close. As he kept her tight to him, he felt a pair of arms around him, arms that stretched around him and touched Hope's shoulders. Hazel Mackintosh's face appeared at his shoulder. Soon, his entire team were around him, some hugging, others simply placing a hand on Hope's shoulder. When the moment had passed, they all stepped away with only Macleod left facing Hope. Stewart then stepped forward, holding a hairband, and pushed back Hope's hair, tying the red mass up behind her in a ponytail.

'Come on, Boss, Ross wants a photo of the day.' Stewart took Hope's hand and she started to lift her up when Hope held up her free hand. Slowly, she let her jacket drop off.

'Can't be seen wearing a duvet, can I? And as for you, sir, none of that old man coat business.' Hope hauled Macleod up and unzipped his coat, leaving him standing in his jumper and shirt. The cold run through him but he was warmed by the smile and laugh of Hope.

When the day was turning to evening, Ross and Stewart packed up the camping table and filled the rucksacks with the rubbish of the day, ready to head back down the hill to the cars. Macleod stood looking out over the firth as his team started to make their way back down and Hazel Mackintosh came up to him.

'You did good, Seoras. The young ones needed this. Things have been a bit brutal of late and they needed a bit of release. You know Hope's going to need a lot more than a good pep talk though, don't you?'

Turning to the woman, Macleod raised his eyes and then looked back to the water far below. 'And when was I ever the home of good pep talks. I get Hope to do them to the teams

209

I'm so poor at them.' He was silent for a moment and then said out to the air before him, 'I got this wrong, Hazel. If it hadn't had been for Hope, Jane would be dead. As it is, she's really struggling. I'm not sure she's got your strength.'

'Listen to you. Will you take some of your own advice, Seoras, and lean? The cancer near killed me, and it sure as hell changed me, but look at me. That bastard stuck me up high and I'm still here. I'm coming right back and so will Jane. And yes, she'll be different but then we're always different, always changing.'

'You don't understand,' said Macleod. 'Hope suffered because I got it wrong, but I can live with that. She's like me, she signed up for this. So did you, but you got a lot more than you ever expected. Jane didn't.'

'But she signed up for you. God knows I wished she hadn't, Seoras, because I would in a flash, but she did. And that's why she'll come through.'

'I don't know if I can put her through this again though, Hazel? Look at me, I'm weary of death. Tired of seeing people broken apart. Maybe I should just go settle down, retire, and stay with her.'

Mackintosh turned away but she left with one comment. There was an air of disgust as she said it and he could feel her disappointment in him. 'Do that, Seoras, and it'll be the death of you!'

Read on to discover the Patrick Smythe series!

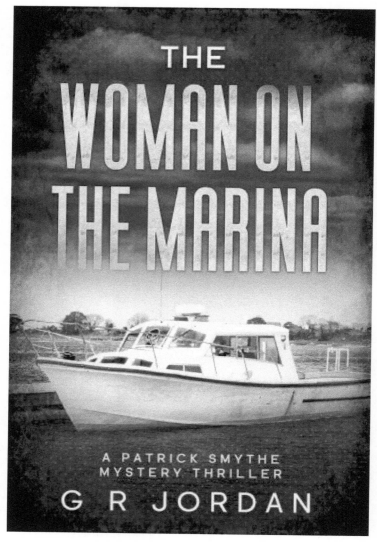

THE

WOMAN ON

THE MARINA

A PATRICK SMYTHE
MYSTERY THRILLER

G R JORDAN

Start your Patrick Smythe journey here!

Patrick Smythe is a former Northern Irish policeman who after suffering an amputation after a bomb blast, takes to the sea between the west coast of Scotland and his homeland to ply his trade as a private investigator. Join Paddy as he tries to work to his own ethics while knowing how to bend the rules he once enforced. Working from his beloved motorboat 'Craigantlet', Paddy decides to rescue a drug mule in this short story from the pen of G R Jordan.

Join G R Jordan's monthly newsletter about forthcoming releases and special writings for his tribe of avid readers and then receive your free Patrick Smythe short story.

Go to https://bit.ly/PatrickSmythe for your Patrick Smythe journey to start!

About the Author

GR Jordan is a self-published author who finally decided at forty that in order to have an enjoyable lifestyle, his creative beast within would have to be unleashed. His books mirror that conflict in life where acts of decency contend with self-promotion, goodness stares in horror at evil, and kindness blindsides us when we at our worst. Corrupting our world with his parade of wondrous and horrific characters, he highlights everyday tensions with fresh eyes whilst taking his methodical, intelligent mainstays on a roller-coaster ride of dilemmas, all the while suffering the banter of their provocative sidekicks.

A graduate of Loughborough University where he masqueraded as a chemical engineer but ultimately played American football, Gary had worked at changing the shape of cereal flakes and pulled a pallet truck for a living. Watching vegetables freeze at -40'C was another career highlight and he was also one of the Scottish Highlands "blind" air traffic controllers.

These days he has graduated to answering a telephone to people in trouble before telephoning other people to sort it out.

Having flirted with most places in the UK, he is now based in the Isle of Lewis in Scotland where his free time is spent between raising a young family with his wife, writing, figuring out how to work a loom and caring for a small flock of chickens. Luckily, his writing is influenced by his varied work and life experience as the chickens have not been the poetical inspiration he had hoped for!

You can connect with me on:

🌐 https://grjordan.com

📘 https://facebook.com/carpetlessleprechaun

Subscribe to my newsletter:

✉ https://bit.ly/PatrickSmythe

Also by G R Jordan

G R Jordan writes across multiple genres including crime, dark and action adventure fantasy, feel good fantasy, mystery thriller and horror fantasy. Below is a selection of his work. Whilst all books are available across online stores, signed copies are available at his personal shop.

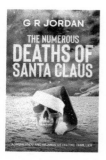

The Numerous Deaths of Santa Claus: A Highlands and Islands Detective Thriller (Highlands & Islands Detective Book 9)
A dead Santa Claus in a garden centre grotto. Underground fighting in the dark corners of the Highlands. Can Macleod and McGrath discover who is dispatching the strongmen of the ring in such a festive fashion?

With Hope McGrath struggling to regain her confidence after a disfiguring injury, Macleod must encourage his protegee as they seek to discover the link between Grotto strangulations and an underground fighting promotion. But as the snow starts to fall and Yuletide celebrations turn sour, Macleod must look beyond the lights and fanciful characters to find the real murderer in their midst.

Ho-Ho-Ho! This time, Santa better watch out!

Highlands and Islands Detective Thriller Series

https://grjordan.com/product/waters-edge

Join stalwart DI Macleod and his burgeoning new DC McGrath as they look into the darker side of the stunningly scenic and wilder parts of the north of Scotland. From the Black Isle to Lewis, from Mull to Harris and across to the small Isles, the Uists and Barra, this mismatched pairing follow murders, thieves and vengeful victims in an effort to restore tranquillity to the remoter parts of the land.

Be part of this tale of a surprise partnership amidst the foulest deeds and darkest souls who stalk this peaceful and most beautiful of lands, and you'll never see the Highlands the same way again.

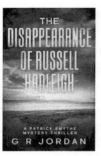

The Disappearance of Russell Hadleigh (Patrick Smythe Book 1)
https://grjordan.com/product/the-disappearance-of-russell-hadleigh
A retired judge fails to meet his golf partner. His wife calls for help while running a fantasy play ring. When Russians start co-opting into a fairly-traded clothing brand, can Paddy untangle the strands before the bodies start littering the golf course?

In his first full novel, Patrick Smythe, the single-armed former policeman, must infiltrate the golfing social scene to discover the fate of his client's husband. Assisted by a young starlet of the greens, Paddy tries to understand just who bears a grudge and who likes to play in the rough, culminating in a high stakes showdown where lives are hanging by the reaction of a moment. If you love pacey action, suspicious motives and devious characters, then Paddy Smythe operates amongst your kind of people.

Love is a matter of taste but money always demands more of its suitor.

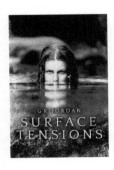

Surface Tensions (Island Adventures Book 1)

https://grjordan.com/product/surface-tensions

Mermaids sighted near a Scottish island. A town exploding in anger and distrust. And Donald's got to get the sexiest fish in town, back in the water.

"Surface Tensions" is the first story in a series of Island adventures from the pen of G R Jordan. If you love comic moments, cosy adventures and light fantasy action, then you'll love these tales with a twist. Get the book that amazon readers said, "perfectly captures life in the Scottish Hebrides" and that explores "human nature at its best and worst".

Something's stirring the water!